Secrets of a Kept Woman

1

SHANI GREENE-DOWDELL

Nayberry Publications | Nayberry Productions

Disclaimer: This manuscript is a work of fiction. It is not meant to depict, portray, or represent any particular persons, living or dead, actual events, establishments, or organizations. Other characters, places, and events are products of the author's imagination and are used fictitiously to give the novel a sense of reality and authenticity. Any resemblances of fictionalized events or incidents that involve real persons are purely coincidental.

Books purchased with a dull or missing cover are most likely stolen and unauthorized by the publisher. Please notify the publisher immediately of where and when you purchased the illegal copy.

Published by Nayberry Publications | 334-787-0733
www.nayberrypublications.com | info@nayberrypublications.com

Edited by Naiomi Pitre | Imoian Press | www.imoianpress.com
ISBN: 978-0981584331
Cover Design Front: Chanel Smith, Web Presence Designs
Cover Design Back: Shani Greene-Dowdell, Nayberry Publications
Copyright 2009, Shani Greene-Dowdell. All rights reserved. The reproduction, transmission, utilization of this work in whole or in part in any form by any electronic, mechanical, or other means, now known or hereafter invented, Including xerography, photocopying, and recording, or in any information storage or retrieval system, is forbidden without written permission. For permission, please contact Nayberry Publications at info@nayberrypublications.com

Acknowledgements

Wow, book three is here! Once again, I reach the juncture in the road where I must stop, reflect, and thank the people close to me as I continue my journey. If you had told me five years ago that I would be a published author typing the acknowledgements for my second full-length novel in 2009 I would have laughed at the thought. Having a dream and determination to see it come to fruition is exhilarating.

I would like to thank my children, Kim, Athena, and Anthony Jr. who are always just as excited as I am when a new book releases. My husband, Anthony Dowdell, Sr. demonstrates tough love that helps to keep me grounded and on the right track. Without my family's support, none of what I attempt to do would be possible, so special thanks to all of my family: my mother, pops, Mom, Madea, my uncles and aunts and extended family who has been nothing but supportive and uplifting.

Finally, I would like to thank my writing community, my Wagfest family. With the support of this group of individuals, I have seen measurable growth in my business and gained an unmatched spirit of extended family like no other. Kerry E. Wagner, Felecia Trotter, Nola Love, you are all the best. Other notable literary friends who have at some point offered inspiration or words of wisdom include Linda Herman, Hazel Mills, Naiomi Pitre, Ivanna Howles, Cydney Rax, and Rukkyah Karreem.

Most importantly, I thank you because you are number one in my book, numero uno, for purchasing or checking my books out from the library faithfully to show faith in my writing. It is you that keeps me going. This read is for you.

Dedication

To any woman that has been heart broken over friendships, love or relationships.

Chapter 1

Sisters From Another Mother

"This side of the equator is hot like fire!" the Channel 3 noonday weatherman said in his update. Tuskegee, Alabama was a southern region of the United States where scorching heat of 103 degrees was a common occurrence. The land was labeled "da blazing durty south," and the summer of 1999 was no different. Warm and muggy weather reflected the mood of the students in Coach Ballard's biology class.

When the three o'clock bell rang, Coach's homework assignments fell on deaf ears. The Booker T. Washington High School students dispersed from their sixth period classes, eager to head home.

"Hey, sit back in your seats until I dismiss you!" he yelled, but there was only one shining star that listened, Shayla Thomas.

She wrote the homework notes in her organizer. Then, she collected her belongings and placed them in her book bag. To be the first one to arrive and the last one to leave was a quality her father taught her. Her grades reflected her dedication.

Coach Ballard walked over to her and placed an arm on her shoulder. "I appreciate your hard work in my classroom, young lady. I noticed your assignments are always on time and the answers are well thought out."

She was happy to be recognized by her favorite teacher. "Thanks Coach. I like science a lot, so doing my assignments to the best of my ability comes natural to me."

"Young lady, you are going places," he said, before walking back over to his desk, closing his planner, and zipping up his brief case.

With a smile, she Shayla exited the classroom. Her teacher's sincerity was encouraging and echoed sentiments she knew to be true. She was going places and going to do big things in her life. She knew as long as she kept her GPA high enough, she was taking one step in the right direction.

Making her way to her locker, she made a mental note to get the books she needed for studying. That next day she had semester exams and quizzes. She collected her textbooks for microbiology, literature, and pre-calculus. She thought about the fact that she had only half a year's worth of gruesome high school work left. She was a young woman ready to leave the drudgery of teenage life behind. After graduation, she planned to enroll in Auburn University's psychology program. Happy was too simple of a word to express how she felt about being accepted into the psychology department's "Student Choice" program.

Having collected what she needed from her locker, she walked briskly toward the bus stop. The last thing she wanted to do was miss her yellow limousine ride home.

"Hey, sistah girl!" Gladys said once she walked out onto the schoolyard.

"Hey, girl," Shayla said as she slowed down to let Gladys catch up with her.

"Did *all* of your teachers assign you a stack of homework for tonight or what?" Gladys asked.

Before Shayla could answer, Ronnie, chimed in. "I told her not to take all of those hard classes, but she's hard headed. We are supposed to be chillaxin' in our senior year, but instead Shayla wants to be Miss Valedictorian."

Shayla's friends gave her a hard time about the time she spent studying each night. Even on Fridays when it was time to hang out, she was glued to her books. She was determined to keep up a four-point-zero GPA.

"I'm taking honors classes. I need the extra time to study," she said.

"I take the same honors classes you do, but my teachers don't give me half as much work. Coach Ballard takes his little science class *too* serious. Aye, Dios mio!" Gladys said.

"And there you go with your Spanglish," Rhonda said. "You know we don't understand that, so speak English please!"

Gladys shot Rhonda a mean look and said, "Shayla's a smart girl. She knows what I said."

"I understand you," Shayla said. "Coach Ballard does give us a lot of work, but science is one of my faves. His class is preparing me for college, and I need all the preparation I can get."

When it came to making the grades, Shayla took pride in cutting no corners. She was going to be the top student in her class, even if it meant studying all night. Gladys wasn't too far behind in the intelligence department, but Rhonda – not so much.

Hoping to encourage her friend, Shayla said, "Ronnie, I'm getting my master's degree, Benz, and three-story house before I turn thirty and I am going to do it all with brainpower. You should join the bandwagon and start working on *your* master plan."

Ronnie opened her mouth to speak and Shayla quickly added, "And a master plan that does *not* include a man.:"

Snapping her fingers, Rhonda spoke as if her words taken from the bible of truths. "You do you! As for me, I will find a man who will do all of the above. Please believe what I say."

"Good luck with that, chica," Gladys said. Her voice dripped sarcasm as she pat Ronnie on the shoulder. "Just get a plan B while you're at it. You may find a papi rico to give you the finer things, mija, but there is nothing like getting your own."

"I got this, tricks!" Ronnie's responded, agitated with the way the conversation was going, so they dropped the subject.

As they walked to the bus stop, Shayla's soft set brown eyes and turned into a frown. She threw her right hand up to protect her eyes from the sunlight.

Rhonda scrunched her nose up as if the heat was causing a stench too strong for her to bear.

Gladys walked ahead of the pack as if the heat didn't bother her in the least bit.

Despite the scorching heat, the friends walked through the schoolyard in a confident strut. They were the perfect trio – one smart, one fiery, and one salsa.

He is riding clean, Shayla thought as she noticed a freshly painted, speckled-gray Cutlass Supreme with limo tint rolling on eighteen-inch McLean wheels.

"Nice ride," Gladys said as the car crept around the corner in slow motion. The music bumped so loud that the noise sent vibrations through the schools' glass windows.

"I bet he has some money, riding clean like that. I wonder who it is?" Rhonda asked.

When the car finally came to a stop, the driver's window slid down and Shayla locked eyes with the driver. He was rocking a LL Cool J style hat. He had skin smooth like butter, luscious lips, and thick eyebrows. His right brow had a distinctive, cute slit down the middle. At the precise moment that his lips turned up into a nice, smooth, LL Cool J smile, all eyes were on him. He could have passed for the rapper's twin. When he looked in the direction of the girls, the full effect of his handsomeness was hypnotic.

Ronnie was the first to break out of her trance. Sounding like Smokey and Craig from the movie,

Friday, she said, "Daaaammmn, he is fine! I'm about to get the 411..." She started sprucing herself up, but stopped when she saw Mr. Jackson walking in the car's direction. "What is Mr. Jackson doing?" she asked as she applied another layer of lip gloss.

Fighting back the dreamy look that threatened to take over her face, Shayla said, "I sure would like to be a fly on the wall."

"That makes two of us," Rhonda said.

"I'm sure he has a girlfriend," Shayla said.

"There you go trying to couple up with a nigga, Shayla. You don't have to 'boyfriend' every guy you think you might like. It doesn't matter if he has a girlfriend, because I'm leaving that marriage and baby carriage for the next chick anyway," Rhonda said, irritated.

"Whatever, Rhonda!"

Rhonda laughed and pushed Shayla out of the way. "Whatever is right."

The gruff assistant principal, Mr. Jackson, fumed as he pointed his finger and scolded the guy in the car. Once the music was off, Mr. Jackson walked away from the car saying, "Don't let me have to tell you about your music again, Mr. Wilson. Do you understand?"

"Yes, Mr. Jackson," the young man said. After Mr. Jackson walked away, Michael Hightower, better known as 'Street Justice,' because of his reputation of being the judge and jury on the streets, trotted up to the car.

Michael had listened to the girls' conversation about the mysterious guy. He said something to the guy and then pointed in the girls' direction. Shayla looked at Ronnie and then to Gladys, shocked. She was even more dumbfounded when Michael jogged back over and addressed her directly.

"My cousin wants you to come over and holler at him, Shay," he said.

"Street, what does he want with me?" she asked, waving him away as if she was not interested. On the inside, she was ecstatic.

She wished she had a mirror to do a quick touch up. A laundry list of nagging thoughts crossed her mind as she thought about approaching him. *Is my hair in place? Do I need a piece of gum? The Thousand Island dressing from my salad at lunch has probably got my breath kicking,* she thought, along with a million other things.

Finally, Street said, "I told him you said that 'I'm sure that fine man is taken, but I want him.'" He laughed at his embellishment of the truth.

"You can't be serious!"

Picking up on Shayla's ambivalence, Michael said, "On the real, just holler at my boy, Shayla. He's good people."

Checking and admiring from the sidelines was her modus operandi, but to actually walk up to a guy and start a conversation was an entirely different ballgame for Shayla. Schoolwork was her expertise. Boys were more complicated.

"Nah, that's okay, Street. Tell him I'll catch him next time," she said.

"Woman up and go handle that," Ronnie said, giving her the quick pep talk she needed to get her confidence level up.

Shayla held her head high as she strutted to the car. "Hey. You wanted me to come speak to you. What's up?" she said once she reached the car.

"Really? I thought you were speaking of me," he said, jokingly raising his sexy left eyebrow. His pearly white teeth flashed brightly and caused her to smile.

"Well, yeah. Actually, we were talking about you when you drove up," she admitted. "But, that was between me and my girls, *not* for Michael to tell you."

"Is that right?" he said, sliding his tongue across his luscious lips once more.

Suddenly, she found her confidence. "Yeah, and you must have liked what you heard and saw, because *you* requested my presence. Now that you have my attention, what's up?"

"You." His answer was simple, but it was game over. She blushed, but she didn't respond. "Since you're holding conversations about me, without including me, you have to give me those digits," he said.

"Is that right?"

"That's right," he said as he fidgeted with his CD changer. Tony Toni Tone's *Just Me and You* played softly through the speakers. "Once I get your number, it will be just me and you on the phone talking."

Cooling the conversation down, Shayla changed the subject. "I see you've turned your music down now. You didn't want Mr. Jackson to kick you off the campus."

"Yeah, Mr. Jackson be tripping, but it's all good."

Just me and you, huh? she thought, as she reached into her purse and tore off a piece of paper from her note pad. She wrote her number down and handed it to him, but snatched the paper back before it was secure in his hands. "Wait a minute. Before I give you my number, at least tell me your name?" She knew it, but she wanted him to introduce himself.

"Titus, but call me Tee."

"Okay, Tee." She put her hand on her hip. "There are a few things I need you to know off the top before I even think about talking to you on the phone. One, you have to treat me like a lady at all times. I'm nobody's bitch or ho..."

The four valuable lessons her father, Rich Thomas, taught her were: One, she was nobody's bitch or ho. Two, never let a man disrespect her. Three, think more of herself than anyone else. Four, trust in a higher power and the rest will fall into place. Those lessons started when she was knee-high and were engraved in her mind. He would say, "You ain't nobody's ho, and I damn sho' ain't raising no punk bitches." Shayla would laugh, but he was as serious as a heart attack.

"Whoooaaa! Wait a minute, baby girl. Pump your brakes. I'm going to give you a phone call. From there, you will have plenty of time to see how well I'm going to treat you as my lady."

"Hmph!" she said and cracked a slight grin. She handed him the note with her name and number.

Titus looked at the paper and said, "Shayla. That's a pretty name." He smiled, and she blushed, once again. "How about I call you tonight around eight?"

She confirmed, "It's a date." She nodded and they parted ways.

On the inside, she melted – not from the sweltering hot summer heat, but from the heat that radiated from Titus to her. He was all that and a bag of chips.

From their small talk, she could tell they would have a great conversation. As soon as she walked off, smiling like she'd hit the lotto, a thick, red-boned chick marched over to his car, arms crossed, and filled with attitude. The girl's curly black weave bounced in the wind as she rolled her neck and engaged in an intense conversation with Titus. She pouted and waved her arms back and forth between her outbursts. Then, she pointed in Shayla's direction and pouted some more.

"What's up with ole' girl?" Ronnie said, rolling up her sleeves. "She doesn't want it with us!"

"Come on, Rhonda, we have to go," Shayla said as she picked up her book bag, took the first step toward her public transportation, and motioned for Rhonda to follow suit.

"Where is Gladys? Did her bus come already?" Shayla asked.

"Yeah," Rhonda said. Her eyes were glued to the female talking to Titus.

"Just let it go, Rhonda," Shayla told her.

Rhonda replied, "For now, but she better not get froggy at school tomorrow."

Chapter 2

A Step Into Womanhood

Later that evening, Titus called Shayla. For hours, they talked about everything under the sun. They spoke about school, life goals, personal interests, and dating. He said the girl that came over to his car and created a scene was his ex-girlfriend.

"I'm not feeling Tammy like that anymore, but apparently she isn't ready to let go," he said.

"Are *you* ready to let go?"

"I *have* moved on, but she is still on some 'We're meant to be together. Let's get married and have a baby,' shit. I'm nineteen. I'm not looking for another mother or a wife. I need someone I connect with."

"I feel you. But, girlfriend was acting like you were cheating on her or something. She is sprung over you," Shayla said and laughed.

"Some females don't know when to let go. They don't know when the relationship is dead. When the lights are out, it's time to put the baby to bed. When the thrill is gone, it's gone."

"And when it's on, it's on, I suppose. Like us?" At that point in the conversation, she didn't care to know the other girl's situation. On the outside, he guy presented himself as the typical thug with brains. On the inside, she discovered a person with a sincere heart.

"Let me pick you up from school and take you home tomorrow. If she doesn't know by now, she'll know tomorrow that I'm digging this certain redbone from around the way," he said.

"Is that right?" she raised an eyebrow as she entwined the phone cord in her fingers.

"Right, and I'm going to show you," he confirmed.

The next day, he picked her up promptly at 3:15 PM. Even though she dodged several eye daggers as she approached his car, she was happy to see him turn the corner. He hopped out of the car, gave her with a single long-stemmed rose, and opened the door for her.

Tammy's expression was so priceless when she saw Titus give Shayla the rose. She could have been bought and sold for a quarter. Shayla and Titus were too caught up into each other to notice the girl running off into the building with one of her friends following close behind.

Over the next couple of weeks, they talked on the phone a lot. They practically shared every detail of their lives with each other. He'd graduated the year before from Booker T. Washington High's rival, South Macon. He lived off J. Anthony Street in the Sloan Mill projects with his family, including three brothers and two sisters. He said college wasn't for him. Even though he didn't go to college, Titus Wilson planned to start his own car dealership, and do something three generations of his family had not been able to do – make it out of the Sloan Mill projects.

Shayla shared her dream of becoming a clinical psychologist and starting her own practice either in Birmingham or in one of the surrounding cities. She knew the dire need for affordable mental health care in Alabama. Watching her mother and brother fight battles with bipolar disease made her more determined than ever to help people suffering with debilitating psychological problems. That was a cause that she was passionate about. At seventeen, she had her life mapped out. By twenty-four, she would be helping the mentally challenged live a better life. By the age of twenty-eight, she'd find the perfect husband. By thirty, she would travel the world over and start a family. Also by that time, she would own a three-story home with a red Corvette sitting beside the latest sport-style Mercedes in her four-car garage.

She had not come from much, but her goals for a picturesque future were far bigger than what she could see with her eyes. When her grandmother told her, "If you work hard to overachieve, Sweet Pea, everything you desire in this world will be at your fingertips," she took those words to heart.

As far as her relationship with Titus, things were going so well that after a few months the duo had gone on a few dates, spoken on the phone at all times of night, and she even skipped school a few times to hang out with him. They were inseparable. Seeds of puppy love were planted. History was in the making. On her graduation night, she gave to him her most precious gift – her virginity. When they left her graduation party, they could barely keep their hands off each other. When they consummated their relationship by making love, he had no doubt in his mind he wanted Shayla on his side as his main girl, and Shayla loved the idea of spending the rest of her life with him.

That next morning, she had to talk to someone, so she called Rhonda to tell her about her night with Titus.

"Girl, last night everything was so special. Titus bought me roses, a necklace, and a ring!" she told Rhonda when she answered on the third ring.

Rhonda said, "You finally gave up the cookie, huh?"

"Yeah, and it was so nice!"

"Do tell." Ronnie said.

"Besides the fact that I love him like my next breath, all I can say is that man is everything! Can you say three snaps in a circle? That man... that man!" Shayla stopped, as if the sheer memory of the prior night had taken her on a ride.

"Oh, you are going to have to give up the goods! Give up the goods." Ronnie said impatiently.

"Okay, so we drove to the Hilton in Montgomery, right?"

"Uh, huh," Rhonda said.

"The hotel was nice. He had the room decorated with rose petals on the floor and bed. Candles were *everywhere* and, chile, he even had a bottle of champagne. He took his time with me. Well, he had to, you know, since it was my first time. He made love to every inch of my body. Treated me like I was the most important woman in the world. I've never experienced anything like it, *ever.* I think I love him. No, I know I love him. He's going to be my husband, girl! I just know it."

"Wait a minute, girl. Wait a minute." Rhonda was at a loss for words as she put Shayla on hold. She dialed Gladys' number and connected her into the call.

"This is too juicy. I had to get Gladys on this call. Gladys, Shayla don' let Titus pop her cherry and now she's talking about marrying him. Tell Gladys what you told me, but start from the beginning," Rhonda said, sounding excited for her friend.

"Mija, what could possibly have you talking marriage after one night of 'love making'. You didn't even know what you were doing," said Gladys.

Shayla started from the beginning, inviting her friends into the most intimate evening of her life – the night she had become a woman.

Chapter 3

Shayla

Eleven Years Later

"I love him too much to let go," I said as I paused a moment to take in the sensual and alluring ambience set for the evening. The statement pounded into my head like a meat cleaver. The strongest thud pulsated against my temple, sending a pain from my head through my body. That pain took up residence in my heart, piercing my already fragile soul. My mind raced. I was all alone, again. I couldn't pin down the moment in time that the insatiable joy left our marriage. That joy slipped away from our beautiful home without leaving the faintest trace of existence.

After six years of marriage, I wondered what was the use of having it all, if I didn't have anyone to share it with. It was an absolute wonder how time, a whole lot of trials, and many tribulations could change a woman's outlook on life and love. The day I married Titus, I was so happy. Our relationship was far from perfect, but I loved him so much.

"This yard is beautiful," I said as I looked around at the beautiful setting once again. I was proud to have successfully turned my backyard into a lover's paradise. Positioned in the middle of the jumbo gazebo, the Jacuzzi flowed with warm bubbly water scented with a touch of jasmine oil. Dim post lighting outlined the gazebo creating a glowing allure. Pink floating candles shone brightly at the gazebo's four corners and an assortment of designer candles placed around the Jacuzzi added the right effect. I anticipated a beautiful night with him. That anticipation dwindled and finally fizzled out once the champagne got hot, the shrimp fettuccini got cold, and every bubble in the Jacuzzi fizzled down to faint traces of soap scum.

What was supposed to be a night of fiery passion turned into a night of me singing, "What do the lonely do?"

Instead of wallowing in my sadness, I called Rhonda to vent. I picked up the cordless phone and sped-dialed her number. Anger built as I walked outside.

"Ronnie, this negro has done it again!" I fumed as I cleared unused dishes from the picnic table. I took them into the kitchen.

"Girl, don't start. What is it now?"

"He stood me up. That's what."

"I can't believe that."

"Yeah and he's not even answering his cell, now." As I spoke the words to my sister-from-another-mother, I fought back a tear that kept threatening to break out of its prison of pride.

"He's probably just busy, Shay."

"If I wasn't wearing his ring on my finger, I would think I was just some sideline ho trying to get attention." Aside from the ring and living with him, that was how I felt. He hadn't been home for more than a few hours that week. He hadn't made love to me in over a month. I hadn't had a meaningful conversation with him in just as many days. Three days ago, he called to schedule tonight's date, which he didn't show up for.

"I can't believe I fell for his lies again, Ronnie." My hands shook as I poured a glass of wine. I took a long swig of the drink and leaned back against the kitchen counter. "I mean, who am I kidding? He rarely comes home, and when he does, it's for less than an hour or two at a time. This marriage is basically over."

"Hang in there, sister," Ronnie encouraged. "Things may get better."

"I love him. You know that, but I can't continue like this. I will *not* sit around here waiting for him night after night as my clock runs out. I'm twenty-eight years old, and I'm not getting any younger. Thirty is knocking on my door."

Rhonda made a valiant, yet unsuccessful, attempt to cheer me up. With a smile in her voice, she said, "Well, look at the bright side, girl. Thirty *is* the new twenty."

"I ain't falling for that!" I slammed the empty glass on the kitchen island. "Thirty is *not* the new twenty. Girl, go check that mirror one more time. We do not look twenty." The mention of my age made me feel worse. If the next six years of my marriage would be anything like the first six, I looked forward to being a bitter, 34-year old woman. At that point, I lost my battle with that stubborn tear. It drizzled down my right cheek and fell onto the carpeted floor, alongside my pride and self respect. If my father saw me then, he would have been so disappointed. I couldn't believe how far gone I was for a man who somehow managed to inspire me to reach for the stars only to shoot my rising star down.

I rearranged and reorganized my goals to accommodate his. He successfully stole my heart and, then like a thief in the night, he was gone without a trace. In the short time we were together, I managed to break off nearly every tie to the outside world. I put things I wanted to do with my life on hold.

My dream of being a clinical psychologist was shelved as I helped him grow his business. When he made his first million, he said, "No wife of mine will be working." So, at his persistence, I settled into the role of a pampered housewife. I settled, because I believed in his promise that once the day came when his money was good I would go back to school.

I rarely visited my family. My mother didn't like the hold he had on me and when mother didn't like someone it was a given that the rest of the family would despise them, as well. Without her approval, no one made it in or out of the family. That was the way it was, until I defied that unspoken rule by marrying Titus anyway. Despite her bipolar illness, she had the presence of mind to know that he would put me through hell. It was more than she was willing to sit back and watch as a bystander. When my father suffered a heart attack four years ago, mother was distraught. She became persistent that I could do better for myself. She didn't want to see stress eat me alive, like it had my father.

I walked over to the glass mirror hanging on our kitchen wall. It revealed a reflection I wasn't prepared to see. *Mama is always right,* I could hear her vivid words playing out in my mind.

My image forced me to put more stock in the meaning of the words. My petite frame was devoid of the beautiful spirit that once dwelled within it. My eyes were cold and unreadable. My lips were pouty, pale, and puffy. My hair, though healthy and glowing from the best care money could buy, was disheveled. The pretty caramel skin that covered my flawless face was flushed red from anguish. Not only had Titus stopped loving me, I stopped loving myself.

Thank God I had Rhonda's shoulder to cry on. She listened to me. There were no judgments passed. She was there any time I needed her, lending me her time and support unselfishly, as she had consistently done the entire six years of my marriage.

The streets helped Titus make good on his promise to be the first one in his family to make it out of the hood. He dabbled on the wrong side of the law in pharmaceuticals and ran operations in practically every hood in east Alabama. The same streets that keep generations of his family's spirits broken and in despair were the same streets that catapulted him to his millionaire status. Once money piled up and we were financially able to live every dream we had ever dreamed, he forgot about me. It slipped his mind that it was me that stood by his side when it was all just a pipe dream.

I had so much on my mind. Rhonda snapped me back to the ever so palpable present when she said, "Shayla, are you still there? Shay-la!"

"I'm here," I assured her.

"Are you going to be okay over there, honey?"

"I will be all right. Just thinking about how different things would be if he…." I stopped mid-sentence. I could not bring myself to think the thought that my husband didn't love me anymore.

Rhonda sighed. "If he what?"

God knew I loved me some Ronnie, but she was single. Sometimes, she just didn't understand me. Gladys would have been more sensitive to my situation; however, she was unavailable. After receiving an invitation to a masquerade ball from her old college buddy, Brenda Jackson, Gladys skipped town without a second thought. In desperate need of a getaway, she found the nerve to take a trip to Miami without her husband or kids. I was sure that her husband, James, was losing his mind. But, she was my shero for making that move. If only I had the nerve to do something for and about me for once. At that precise moment, I smiled with a glimmer of joy for her.

The thought crossed my mind to bust up her vacation with my problems. Then, I decided against it. It wasn't like I had anything new to tell her. Just the same-ole-same-ole 'Titus won't come home' story. I could hear what she would say, 'Love it or leave it, chica." Her stance on me staying with Titus was to take what he had to offer but make it work for me.

One thing that hadn't changed after all of these years was that I trusted both of my girls with my life. I knew that no matter what, they had my best interest at heart. We went through a lot together. Our friendship was paramount.

Chapter 4

Shayla

As I continued to vent to Rhonda, I could hear her brushing her fingernails against her nail file. She either rolled her hair between her fingers or filed her fingernails when she was in deep thought, so I knew she was just as stressed out as I was. As far back as I could remember, no matter what Titus did, she had never spoken a bad word about him. She liked his 'rough around the edges' style and was impressed with the money he made. The fact that he was from the streets was a plus, in her book. His ability to take care of me was something that she admired. She loved Titus like a brother, so I knew she wanted to see our marriage survive. That was just how real of a friend she was.

"Ronnie, I guess we did all of this for nothing," I told her, feeling hurt and ashamed that we spent hours shopping and preparing the backyard earlier that day.

I thanked God for her, as most of the decorations came at her suggestion. I looked longingly out of the sliding glass doors to the intimately decorated, lakeside yard. Our Victorian-style house was positioned on the most prime real estate in Pine Mountains. The sight was a bit too much for me to digest at that moment, so I turned my back on it. Immediately, unwanted memories of my fifth wedding anniversary rushed upon me. Last year, the week before my anniversary, Ronnie and I took a vacation in Maui – just us girls. Upon returning home, I was pleasantly surprised to be welcomed by Titus holding a blindfold.

My husband held me tightly around the waist and led me into my new completely renovated kitchen. Everything was done with French style décor, including the best stainless steel appliances. I walked around turning on the oven and other gadgets. I was so filled with joy that my sentimental butt cried for the next hour. He knew that I loved to cook, so the fact that he upgraded the kitchen with the best was the gift of the decade.

What a difference a year makes.

"It's all good. I will do anything to help you," Rhonda said, interrupting my flashback. "But, don't be so upset with Titus. You know he has to be out there making things happen, so you can live the way you do. Either he will make money and bring it home to you, or it will be the next chick that gets it. 'Cause we both know he ain't about to stop making money. Shit, I wish I had a man like that." Rhonda loudly popped the bubble gum in her mouth, and asked, "Don't you like living on Society Shores?"

"I do, but that doesn't change the fact that he needs to behave like a husband. How he only comes to visit every now and then. It is more like I'm his mistress than his wife."

Was I asking for too much? Dare I even say, I longed to share a few laughs, dreams and ideas with the man I loved. I needed him to talk to me about current events for a few minutes out of each day. As a woman with emotional, mental, and physical needs, it was a necessity that I reconnect with my husband, and fast. Either that connection would be established, or I was setting myself free.

I said in all sincerity, "I would give all this up in a heartbeat. I'm ready to start a family, engage in long late night conversations about everything and nothing at all, spend hours staring into his eyes for no reason except that I love the glow in them, and go on family trips and vacations. Sometimes when I'm alone in this big house, I can just imagine the little pitter-patter of baby feet. I wish..." I paused, unable to say the words that would cut through my ego like a knife. Glancing at the ceiling, I attempted to ward off more tears. I cursed the fact that I could be so sensitive. What I wouldn't give to be a hardcore chick that could not only survive, but thrive, in this environment.

"Okay! Okay!" Ronnie broke the silence. "I wasn't supposed to tell you, but maybe, just maybe, he's stuck in Atlanta traffic. He went there today to pick up a gift he had special ordered for you. Dang, now that the cat is out of the bag, do you feel better?"

"Really, he's in Atlanta buying me a gift?" My heart lurched with relief. I wondered why Rhonda would let me go through such anguish when she knew where my husband was.

"Girl, yeah, a sistah's word." A sistah's word was a saying we had for a statement that was the truth. In other words, what she was saying was one hundred percent.

"I know you were trying to keep the surprise, but you could have saved me a lot of grief by spoiling that one, girl. How could you allow me to wallow around whining on the phone for the last hour when you knew that my husband was out picking up a gift? I'm beginning to think you enjoy my pain," I said with a laugh. Despite my unease, I had to admit that my mood brightened at the mere thought of Titus doing something special for me.

"He asked me to keep it a secret," Rhonda said.

I blew my nose into the big wad of tissue I was carrying around with me. Through a stuffy nose, I said, "Okay, you are forgiven."

"He put that ring on your finger, so stop worrying about what he is doing. He should be home soon," Rhonda assured.

I remembered when he proposed. It was the day I walked across the stage to get my college diploma at Auburn University. When the dean called my name to come up and receive the well-deserved master's degree in psychology, Titus called my name on a bullhorn. As everyone searched the audience for the source of his voice, each of his homeboys held up a fluorescent letter that spelled out the words, "MARRY ME SHAYLA." After reading the words, our eyes locked, and he stood there on the sidelines with the biggest, cutest grin on his handsome brown face. In his hand, he held a black velvet box. With my heart full and head swirling, I took the degree papers from the dean and ran over to hug the man I would be spending the rest of my life with.

Once I reached him, I said, "Yes... yes... yes! I will marry you, if you promise to always love, honor and respect me."

Daddy's lessons were still embedded in me, then. I felt like the most special woman in the world when Titus looked into my eyes and said, "Woman, how could I not respect you for your beauty, intelligence, and elevating me to heights no other woman could? I love you, Shayla."

Not only had I received the first college degree in my family, but I had someone special to share my dreams with. He wrapped his arms around me and the warmth of his kiss embraced me. The quick trip down memory lane reminded me of how much I loved that five-foot-eleven, bow-legged, muscular in all the right places, pretty brown-skinned brother. Dried tears on my cheeks cracked as a genuine smile crept up on my face. I told Rhonda, "I love that man. Thanks for always being there for me. You always help me come back to reality."

"You are welcome. I'll always be here for you."

I took a look around at all the expensive things that I couldn't make love to, laugh at a funny joke with, or sit beside on the couch to watch a comedy show with.

When it was all said and done, I couldn't get any love from the chinchilla coat or Chanel pumps. The whole ordeal had me completely drained. I walked through the kitchen into the den and sat on the plush leather sofa. Its warmth and comfort provided intimacy.

"Between me and you, last week I was so horny I thought about getting my creep on. If I didn't have every eye in town watching me, I swear my groove would be back by now. Not saying cheating is what I want, but a woman has needs," I confided.

"Don't get drastic! You know he is a fool over you. Just give him a chance to explain why he is late tonight," Rhonda calmly spoke up in Titus' defense.

"How can he explain, if he won't answer his phone? I called his cell fourteen times today and guess what?"

"He didn't answer?"

"Bingo!" I stretched out on the sofa and stared at the ceiling while I held the phone to my ear.

"Yes, but think about the end, when he doesn't have to hustle like this anymore. You're already living larger than you'd ever imagined. Remember in high school when you said that by thirty you would have a three-story home with a Denali sitting beside the hottest sports car in your four-car garage?"

"Yes, I remember that. I also said that by thirty, me and my perfect hubby would have traveled the world over and would start working on a family. A lot has changed since high school."

"Okay, well, you'll be able to appreciate those long trips and long hours away from home when your pockets blow up like an atomic bomb. Start a family and travel the world on that!"

If I knew one thing for sure and two things for certain, Rhonda could see good in everything Titus did. She was part of the reason I put up with him as long as I had. That and the fact that he would probably kill before he let me go.

"Well, girl, I'm going to let you go. No need in both of us having a depressing Friday night," I said.

"Imagine that." Ronnie laughed.

"Whatever. I'm sure you're about to get your club on or do something fun."

"No, actually sweetie, I had a little company earlier, so I'm going to be getting some much needed rest."

"Anyone that can keep 'Ronnie the Diva' away from Club Diamond on a Friday night must be the-man-twenty-grand." We both laughed at my corny joke. Rhonda began to speak, but I cut her off. "Let me guess. Is it Curtis Jackson?"

Instead of answering the question, Ronda sighed exhaling a long breath.

"Well, don't be all secretive. Give up the goods, who is he? Do I know him?"

"Let's not get into all that, Miss Thang. I will tell you all about him soon enough. Listen, I'll talk to you tomorrow," Rhonda said after a yawn.

"Cool, we'll just..." I started to say we'll talk tomorrow, but the dial tone blaring through the phone stopped me mid sentence. I pressed the button to turn off the phone and wondered what could be up with

Rhonda. Her sudden shortness was odd. I chopped it up as her being tired.

I had my own problems to deal with, like Mr. Wilson and his whereabouts.

Chapter 5

Rhonda

I hung up the phone with Shayla and decided to indulge in round two with the fine specimen sleeping like a baby in my bed. Leaving my lacy red two-piece lingerie ensemble on the bedroom floor, I headed for a quick shower. After showering with my favorite vanilla shower gel and softening my mocha colored skin with a delicate lotion, I headed back into the bedroom. I eased over to the bed with the sensuality of a lioness. Starting at his chest and working down to his feet, I massaged him gently. A broad naughty smile spread across my face and I knew he was ready. No man could resist the power of my touch.

Akin to an act of nature, he reached up and cupped my breasts, one in each hand. Heat radiated from his touch. The moment was perfect, until he spoke the words that broke the mood. “I gotta get going. What time is it, Ronnie?”

With a feline whisper into his Burberry-scented earlobe, I said, "Time for round two."

His manhood came to a peak under the silken sheets, letting me know he wanted me too. I laid next to him on my back and gently took his right hand into mine, guiding it to the wetness between my thighs. I would've given my last dime for him to fill the void between my thighs.

His face followed the wetness. "I see lil' mama still wet for Daddy," he said as he flickered his tongue across my swollen lips before inserting his tongue deep into my love. "You tastin' good, too."

I felt the brink of an orgasmic wave coming down when he stopped and smacked me hard on the thigh.

"What you stop for?" I asked, feeling like I needed an orgasm more than I needed air to breathe.

"I gotta go. I got shit to take care of."

"But..." Instead of flipping out like I wanted to, I did the only thing I thought would make him stay. I begged. "Please, stay a little while longer. Make love to me one more time. Please stay. I love you."

"I was just teasing with ya' ass. You know how I do," he said flippantly, as he fidgeted around until he found his pants. He retrieved his cell phone out of his pocket and turned the phone on. "Fourteen missed calls! Shit! You were supposed to wake me up at eight. It's 9:45!" He jumped up. Before I could respond, he gathered his clothes off the floor and rushed into the bathroom, closing the door behind him.

I knew where he had to go, which was exactly why I intentionally let him oversleep in the first place. It was supposed to be a special night for my best friend and her husband, but I wanted him to stay with me.

Earlier that day, I helped Shayla's pathetic ass shop for their dinner, candles, negligee, and the whole nine yards. It was actually quite fun shopping with her, knowing the whole time that he would be in my bed.

As soon as she let me know she planned to rekindle something special with Titus, I knew I had to infiltrate.

If I had anything to do with it, it would never happen. Shayla, rekindling a romance with a man that rightfully belonged to me? That would be a negative.

Just minutes ago, she was on the phone pouring her sweet little heart out about him. She probably spent many nights making the difficult choice of which vibrator to use and I could care less. I even helped her 'need some love' butt pick the dildos out. I swear, she could be so pathetic.

If years of friendship went down the drain over Titus, then so be it. I loved him with all that I had to love. Don't get me wrong, I loved Shayla like a sister, but I felt like vomiting in my throat every time I watched him cater to that bitch. The concern and care he displayed for 'his wifey' was sickening. His affection belonged to me and it was high time he figured out that a gangsta needed a down ass chick on his team, not a whiny ass wife that was always talking about her feelings and shit.

In a world so cold, all that feelings could get you were a wet pussy and a broken heart, or even worse... dead. Sure, I didn't like standing around in the background getting leftover scraps. Yet, I gave in to the understanding that having part of him was better than nothing at all.

"I want you, right now, Titus!" I directed the words toward the bathroom door, knowing he couldn't hear me with the shower running. He would never agree to leave her, yet he deserved so much more. Only a woman in my position would understand the frustration of knowing he has deep and inexplicable love for someone else when I'm the one that can give him everything he needs.

All through high school, the boys I crushed on pursued Shayla. Because of her light skin and naturally curly hair, the guys loved her. She had that Halle Berry look, a beauty from birth. I admitted that she flaunted it well. Though we were thick as thieves, a tiny part of me envied the fact that she attracted guys just by walking in the room. That envy festered within the pit of my soul until I acted on it by fucking the one person she loved, Titus. It wasn't like he was the first one of her boyfriends that I crept with. In the 11th grade, I broke off preppy ass Carlton Levette a little sum'n sum'n right under the bleachers during the homecoming game. While Shayla was on top of the world performing the halftime routine, Carlton brought his A-game performance on top of me.

Having Carlton scream out, "Ronnie… Oh, Ronnie!" right there in the middle of the game was the most gratifying experience I ever had at that point in my life. It was my way of proving that I could outdo her, even if it was just by out-sexing her man. I wanted a piece of her world, so I used what I had to get what I wanted. It was as simple as that.

Unlike Shayla, I gave men what they needed. In return, Titus made sure I was well taken care of with money, cars and anything my pretty little head could dream up. He told me that as long as I kept our rendezvous our little secret, he would keep my pockets lined and my bed warm. That was a happy arrangement for me, until that night. I'd have been damned if I was going to wake him up to go home and lay in a scented Jacuzzi, sip champagne and make love to her.

I didn't have the seventy-five-hundred square foot Victorian home, my choice of luxury cars, and the black Visas that Shayla had the luxury of possessing. I also doubted very seriously that he stood around fussing at her over my missed calls. But, as far as I was concerned, those things were about to change real soon.

Chapter 6

Titus

Within five minutes, I showered and was fully dressed. Standing in front of Ronnie, I was hotter than a firecracker with her sexy ass. I wanted to slap the taste out of her mouth, but I let her slide for not waking me up on time. I knew beneath her hard exterior, she was just in puppy love with a nigga, man. She played hard, but her feelings were wrapped up in this so-called relationship. I guess some folks would call this a relationship, but having another wifey was exactly what I didn't need. To me, she was something to do. In the beginning, she said she felt the same way. But, I'd been in the game too long to believe that. Wrapping my arms around her tight enough to let her know she was fucking with a real nigga, I squeezed that ass one more time before I left. I pulled out a stack of cash and left it on her nightstand.

"Keep it tight for me, Ronnie!" I said and smacked her hard on the ass. "I'm the only one that can hit that, so don't make me catch a case. I'ma holla at you later in the week."

Opening the door to her bedroom, I hurried toward the front door. I had to get home. If Ronnie was any of my other women, I swear that I would have slapped her silly ass serious for not waking me up on time, especially since she had no excuse for not doing what she was told. She was a part of my inner circle; however, she was really beginning to test me. I didn't ask my women to do nothing but shop, look sexy, and do whatever the fuck I told them to do. There were two things I didn't deal with well: discrepancies with my time or discrepancies with my money. Up until that day, she hadn't experienced my wrath. When other bitches were foul, they were straight up casualties of war. You can check my dental records and find evidence that Titus Wilson didn't even play the radio!

As I turned the front doorknob, I felt like shit for letting Shayla down again. I was going to have to deal with her attitude when I got home.

Rhonda's soft hand grabbed my arm and jerked me around to face her. "Are you sure you can't just stay, babe?" she asked softly. Tears were rolling down her face. "You can keep the money," she said, sounding pathetic. "I just want you with me. Please don't go running home to her."

I could tell by the look on her face she was speaking out of desperation. She had a rival thing going with Shayla that I didn't think was cute or effective. I didn't have time for her emotional ass. "You know I can't do that," I told her as I checked my Rolex. It read 10:15.

She walked closer to me, put her arms around my neck, looked into my eyes, and gave me that bedroom look that I loved. "We both know that you can do what you want."

I maneuvered her arms from around my neck and stepped back. "You know what the deal is. I have a wife that is waiting for me at home."

"Let's change the deal, then. It can be me and you."

She thought she was about to get me caught up in hours of her whining, but I didn't have time for it. "Look, little mama, I'm a married man. I'm your best friend's husband, not yours. It's bad enough I got to deal with her when I get home."

"But Titus..." she attempted to put her arms back around my neck, but I blocked her that time.

"I don't have time to run down your role to you. Time is money. I have to go." My temper was about to get the best of me. As each second passed, she looked more and more like one of the nagging bitches that I dealt with in the past. How was she going to be the jump off and forget she was the jump off. Ronnie should had been happy she was given as much time, attention, and respect as she was. She forgot who she was dealing with.

"You know the game. Respect the rules," I said, opening the door. I gave her another chance to redeem herself and be the strong woman I knew. Not wanting to be disappointed, I didn't look back when I walked out the door.

She screamed, "Since you want to treat me like I'm a jump off, why weren't you at home with your 'wifey' tonight sipping champagne, laying in the Jacuzzi, and eating the gourmet meal that her pathetic ass spent all evening cooking?"

A part of me said to walk on to the car and go home, but the other part of me thought I had the conversation twisted. Was Rhonda seriously stepping to me with some bullshit? When I didn't respond, she continued screaming.

The second time, she sounded bolder. "If you went home, then maybe she wouldn't be on the phone with me crying her weak little heart out. Seems to me like *she's* been downgraded to the jump off, so let's just keep it real here!"

"What did you just say?" I wanted to hear it again. I had to be sure I wasn't mistaken. Preparing for her to repeat her verbal assault, I bit down on my lip. Hands folded in a knot, I was ready to punch a hole in something.

"You heard me right, nigga! I'm not your jump off. She is the one that is weak and always whining and crying about you. You should hear her."

Ronnie stopped screaming and spoke in her normal voice. "She can't turn you out like I can, Titus. She don't even know how to. That's because we match like peas and butter, baby. You have all you need in a woman right here, so why are you running to her? You haven't touched your 'wifey' in so long she has cobwebs growing between her legs. She's wore out so many vibrators that they are about to start using her for their commercials." Her laugh went from hysterical to wicked.

I could have kicked myself for giving Ronnie ammunition to make a joke out of Shayla. I stood there and allowed her to go as far as she was comfortable going. She was comfortable enough to disrespect me, and my wife. I was cheating, but I loved my wife. So, friend or no friend, I didn't like hearing Rhonda disrespect her like that. The boldness Rhonda had flowing through her veins made me nervous.

"You don't have to say anything, boo," she said as she puffed a cigarette she'd lit. She exhaled the smoke and her words together. "Oh, you didn't know that she calls me whining about her sexless life, trying to figure out what's the latest and greatest in dildos and vibrators." Rhonda was nearly out of breath, wheezing and laughing her butt off before she got a full understanding of the insufficient checks her mouth had already written.

Man, I caught a case of temporary insanity as I grabbed her by the arm and pulled her back into her apartment. Before I even knew what was happening, one hand was wrapped around her throat. I slapped her face from side to side repeatedly with my free hand. It was almost like I was not the one beating her ass. I felt like a bystander watching the assault from the sidelines.

She fell back onto the couch, and I was still holding her neck and slapping her face in between my words.

"What's fu... funny now? I'm sure you can squeeze one more joke out of that smart-ass mouth of yours. Sure you can. Go ahead – talk."

"T....T...itus!" she attempted to speak, but the hold I had on her jaw wouldn't let the words escape.

"You're hur...ting mmmmeeee... ," she managed to say.

"You think you got the only hot pussy in town? I can have any woman I want. I only messed with you to prove that you were scandalous. I kept coming back because you are good at what you do. Other than that... naw, there is no other than that. I told you that Shayla is off limits. Let me catch one feeling you told her anything out of the way and you will hate the day you ever met me."

I didn't want to kill her, but my killer instinct had kicked in. I could see her gurgling and foaming at the mouth, and the color started to leave her dark skin. As she went limp, the exasperation in her reddened eyes jarred me back to reality. I quickly released her neck.

She immediately fell off the sofa onto the floor like a rag doll. I stood there watching her gasp for air until the color returned to her face. I almost felt bad for what I did, but quickly reverted to street principle # 79 – Act like a lady, and you get treated like a lady. Run up, and get done up. It was hard but fair.

Rhonda lay on the floor looking like a fool gasping for air. It served her right. She wanted to live a gangsta life. She wanted to be hard. Then, she might as well take the hard knocks like a gangsta bitch. I was Titus-to-the-motherfucking-Wilson. I walked down her hall and back into the bedroom, picked up the money I placed on the nightstand earlier and put it back in my pocket. Until she got her act together, she would not be living on my dime.

"Playing with my livelihood, toying with my emotions is a mistake. You forced me to show you how real it can get. You know me well enough to know that you chose the wrong one to try to man handle. Act like a lady, and you'll get treated like a lady," I said before I dusted myself off and walked to the door.

I heard her say, barely above a whisper, "How could you do this to me, Titus? I thought you loved me."

I didn't know how she thought I loved her. I never told her that. Sure, I spent a lot of time with her, but I never told her I loved her. It was time for me to let Ronnie know she really didn't come first in my life. Truth be told, something about messing around with my wife's best friend that had me a little open. Forget that, let me keep it real for a second. *Ronnie* had me wide open. The sneakiness involved with our fling made experiences with her erotic as hell. Plus, she really cared and looked out for a nigga, man. That alone had me feeling a certain kind of way for her. All the nights I came home and was greeted by Shayla and Rhonda finally piqued my interest of getting with her. I would have suggested a threesome, but Shayla would have flipped.

For two whole years, she had me paying all of her bills and spending mad time with her. But, Rhonda's jealousy and disrespect closed that door as quickly as it opened. She was right about one thing; it was time I tended to Shayla's needs. I had to let Ronnie go.

"I'm going to miss that good loving though," I said to myself while getting into my car. "Damn, that girl can do some things in bed." Anything I suggested, she was down with it like it was the way life was supposed to be.

On the other hand, my sweet and loving Shayla was far too precious for that. I made tender love to her. Wifey brought out a different energy from me that inspired me to explore her in different ways than I did with any of my other women. It was like I melted into her sweet pussy. All the veins in my forehead came to the surface, my arms shook as they held me up, and I wished I could dive in and come out the other side of that thing when I made love to her. One session with her and she had me ready to give up the whole street game and settle down. She had the power to inspire me, not only give her the best, but to be a better man. That was why I married her, but also why I spent so much time away from her. I wasn't ready to be a square – cooking meals, painting walls, watching the Home Makeover channel on TV, and eating ice cream sandwiches as the highlight of my day.

Ever since the day I made it down the aisle with Shayla, I'd been running from the lockdown. I was afraid of turning into a sap, making love and shit. For one, I was afraid of the hold she had on me. In my line of work, I had to keep it gangsta by any means necessary. The streets would eat me alive on some love bullshit. For two, I wasn't sure I dismissed the fact that I liked to be out there being "the man" to other females.

I wanted it all – wife, security, money, and other women.

Picking up my phone, I called home and got our voicemail. “Shayla, baby, I’m sorry I missed your calls. I’ve been tied up handling a discrepancy. I’m on my way home now. I love you.” I said a prayer she would receive my message before I got there and not be too upset. I looked in the rearview mirror, and said, “Pimpin’ ain’t easy.”

Chapter 7

Gladys

Flashback: Matrimonial Bliss

It is our sixth month anniversary, and I am probably being sentimental and silly, since most people only celebrate their yearly anniversaries, but I don't care. I love this man, and right now, he needs me more than ever. He was demoted from his position as a manager at J-Plex Department Store last week, and I want to cheer him up. As his esposa neuva (his new wife), I want him to know I am here for him. I want his smile back. That is what I fell in love with about him, after all.

I dropped rose petals all the way from our bedroom to the kitchen table. I am standing over the kitchen stove preparing his favorite breakfast. As he walks into the kitchen, I am just about to place freshly prepared turkey sausage on a plate, along with scrambled eggs, grits, and a slice of orange. I have a pitcher of freshly squeezed orange juice on the table and a single vanilla candle burning as the centerpiece. I absolutely beam with pride when I turn around to face my handsome husband. I smile brightly with love radiating from my wide eyes and greet him.

"Good morning, papi! I know you have to be at work in about an hour, but I have cooked some of your favorites. I was hoping that you would have a few minutes, so that we could talk about what has been bothering you." I give him my warmest look and poke out my bottom lip, trying to be as cute as possible.

When James snatches the plate from me, my facial expression drops. Emotionless, he slams it down onto the table, causing the grits to jump and spill over the place. I stare at that huge splotch of grits and, as they sink in deeper to my good tablecloth, I can feel the fear and sadness doing the same within my own heart. Spit flies from his lips as he bellows at me. "Talk, huh? Well, let's talk about the fact that you're fixing me this bullshit to eat for breakfast. Do I look like some kind of dog to you?"

In shock, I take a step back. He has to be joking. I lift my eyes from the table and search within his to try and find a trace of humor lurking there. The look on his face was somber and grim. His eyes look dead and flat. He was definitely not joking. This is a look that is unfamiliar to me. I am confused.

Flustered, I answer, "No, James, and you know I don't think you are a dog. I... I was just trying to ... Why would you ask me a question like that?"

"Because, Gladys," He spat my name as though it were acid on his tongue. "You're fixing something that looks like dog food, bitch! I know you think you're better than me because you've got your little job as a computer tech, but I'm nobody's dog!" As he shouts at me, he takes steps closer and closer until our noses are an inch apart. I can smell the Cool Mint Listerine on his breath, and the Cool Water Cologne on his neck, but his temper is anything but cool. Did he just call me a puta? No one in my entire life had ever called me that. I must have heard him wrong. I had to have. I mentally curse the day I told him about my promotion. Ever since, he has been in a pissy mood. Then, his demotion comes at the absolute worst time.

I don't recognize mi esposa, at all. The expression on his face makes him look as though he is possessed by Lucifer, or el Diablo, himself. I can't pretend to be strong. His attitude completely takes me off guard, after I spent all morning thinking he would be thrilled by my hard work. I imagined he would sweep me off my feet, swing me around the kitchen, and maybe even take me right here on the dining table. Instead, here I am, face to face with a beast I didn't know resided within him.

A flame of fear travels through my bones, and I begin to shake. The fright is so overwhelming I almost gag.

"What the fuck are you giggling about, you Spanish whore. You think I'm a fuckin' joke?"

"Oh my god, James, I wasn't laughing at you. I... I... I don't know what has gotten into you this morning, but you need to..."

WHOP!

The next thing I know, I am half-way across the room holding my left cheek, which is screaming in excruciating pain. My back hurts like hell from the violent contact with the corner of the countertop on my way to the ground.

"Don't you ever tell me what you think I need to do, Gladys! I'm a man! I do what I want to do," he screams.

My eyes follow him. I wonder who is this monster that has taken over my James' body? He never so much as raised his hand to me in the entire two years that I had known him. Hurt to the core, my heart bleeds twice as heavy as my face. I sit on the floor too emotionally paralyzed to move. There is no way I am a battered woman. I am not like the other women I've always talked about. I felt sorry for those women who couldn't be strong enough to leave those horrible husbands. I always thought they were weak and much more vulnerable than me. Es muy imposible! No freaking way am I about to accept the title of being a victim of domestic violence. I find the strength to ask, "James, how... how could you dare hit me? What has gotten into you?"

James storms out of the room hollering, "What has gotten into me, you ask? No senorita! It is what is about to get into you."

I am relieved that he is no longer in the same room. After hearing him scrambling through our bedroom closet, I cringe as he returns. He walks briskly toward me. I am still sitting on the floor, curled into a fetal position. I try to melt into the wall. I want to be invisible, so I won't have to face him again. I don't know who this woman is as she holds onto her elbows and rocks back and forth. I cry for the pain I am feeling – inside and out. I cry for my marriage. I cry for every woman who has ever suffered domestic violence.

"You are about to learn some respect, woman." The calmness in his voice inspires even more fear than his outraged yelling. It is then I realize he has his thick belt wrapped around his hand. When his intentions dawn on me, I forget my proud Spanish upbringing and plead with him for mercy. Briefly, visions of my father lecturing me when I was a little girl about having respect for myself so that others will respect me float into my thoughts. The seriousness of the situation at hand pushes those thoughts away. I hold my hands out to him and beg for my life.

"No! James, please no!" I scream at the top of my lungs, or at least it seems to me as if I am

screaming loud, but only hoarse whispers are heard. As the belt swings in a wide arc over his head, I cry out, hoping to touch any warm-blooded place left in his heart. The belt makes its way closer to my body, again, and I whisper helplessly, "Please... don't hit me again..."

It was only after six measly months of marriage when my matrimonial bliss turned into a den for the devil's work. It seemed the only thing James had going for him were the three "A's": anger, aggression, and adultery. If people knew what I was going through behind the uniquely designed doors of our home, they would think I was gullible and naïve for falling in love with someone like him in the first place. In actuality, he used to love me and show me the utmost respect. He put me first, and my family liked him enough to put up every dime for our wedding. It was extra money that they did not have.

How could I go back to my father and tell him that the twenty thousand he took from his hard-earned retirement account was in vain, because the man that I married was beating me? I wouldn't be his prized princesa bonita anymore. I would be a disgrace to my family. My father would disown me. I couldn't bear to think of the look on his rugged, hardworking face if he would ever find out.

Since that first beating, James' modus operandi was to verbally attack me and intimidate me into a shivering heap of tears so badly that he didn't even have to beat me in order to get me to submit to whatever he wanted. Certainly, he was not above putting his hands on me, but the beatings were not as frequent. I lived through the worst of it for the past six years with him – the absolute worst. We kept up a good public face, though. To see us out and about, you would think that we were just as in love as we were in college.

I moved to America with my family when I was fourteen in search of endless American possibilities. Therefore, I had the benefit of speaking both Spanish and English. I lived in Valley, Alabama in a nice, custom-built four-bedroom brick home. I commuted daily to Naytek's office in the bustling downtown Atlanta. Although I could have lived in Atlanta, I chose to commute to the smaller, modest community of Valley, because James and I enjoyed the countryside. Small town life matched my serene, simplistic lifestyle.

I hadn't even told my best friend what was happening to me at home. I was the type of woman that didn't have many friends. I preferred to have the least amount of prying ears and eyes in the vicinity as possible. The only two people, aside from my family, I kept in close contact with were Shayla and Rhonda.

Well, if I am being honest, there was only really one that I trusted – mi mejor amiga (my best friend), Shayla. Rhonda was the third-wheel to our duo, and I trusted her as far as I could toss her. She was selfish and conceited, as far as I was concerned. I was friends with her more because Shayla always had her around.

It was obvious Rhonda felt the same about me. We were more like friendly enemies, or frenimies. I couldn't remember a specific moment when she was truly there for me, in a best-girlfriend-who-I-would-do-anything-for kind of way. I could rattle off several times Shayla had come through for me.

Sitting at a stoplight, I took a long look at the gold-encrusted special invite to Brenda Jackson's 2009 Grown and Sexy Masquerade Ball in Miami, Florida. It had been a while since I saw my old college friend. I wondered how she found my contact information to have the party planning company personally deliver an invite to my job.

She'd planned a reunion getaway for the graduates of the African American studies program at Albany State, class of 2002. I was ready to reconnect with some of my old friends. To top the reunion off, Brenda hooked me up with two freebie nights at the hotel resort. I wondered what the weekend had in store, but knowing Brenda, it could be anything. Something wild and crazy would be what the doctor ordered. As far back as I could remember, she was the life of the party. In college, it wasn't enough for Brenda to be on the cheerleading squad. No! She was the head of the Honor Society, Ambassador to the United States for the Culture Team America, track star, volleyball star, Spanish Honor Society President, and President of the African-American Study Club. African-American studies was my minor, so I was blessed to meet such a dynamic soul while I was there.

That invitation meant more to me than time to let loose and get buck wild. It was a much-needed time to get away from all of the madness at home.

Almost in Miami, I changed lanes, switching over to the side of traffic that was moving the fastest. I breezed down the highway, anxious to get my weekend kicked off. I couldn't wait to reach my hotel and spend the next two days in another town. For just a hot second, I thought about James and how he must have felt when he came home from work to find my Oh-by-the-way-I'll-see-you-on-Monday letter. I would have paid good money to see the look on his face when my mother brought the kids home at six.

"Ha! I wonder how he liked that!" I laughed, imagining how he screamed. He probably soiled his pants once I called and confirmed that it was not all just some silly joke.

I should have been the one acting a fool, considering the email message I received one Sunday morning from an anonymous woman claiming to have a special relationship with my husband. That same weekend, he had a conference to attend for work.

It was enough that I put up with his abuse, but to receive messages like this from his mistress was just too much. I won't even attempt to explain the childish message from the email address, hiswoman@tmail.com. It read:

Dear Gladys,

Last weekend was absolutely amazing! Saturday, me and James got up and got dressed, then went to the mall for like, two hours. I shopped until I got too tired to swipe his Visa, and then we went to Target and I'm pretty sure we found some stuff we're going to decorate our new house with. Oh yeah, he's leaving you honey, and we are starting a life together, so take this note as a heads up. On the way home, we stopped and ate at that Mexican restaurant you love so much, which was so freaking delicious. The whole day, including us playing tennis for four hours in total, two hours before we left and two when we got back, was beautiful. Then, when night fell, we went to a foam dance, and we won the competition. I danced in foam completely topless with nothing on but some itsy bitsy little shorts. James had so much fun. This morning, I woke up in his arms, again. I live to spend time with him on weekends. He loves spending time with me, so it's obvious I've got something that you don't. Oh, we are about to go eat, play some more tennis, then who knows. Life is good. You can email me back, but I doubt I'll answer! James and I will be out enjoying our time together. I love him, so move over.

Forever His Woman

When thinking about that woman's message, Dr. Phil's wise words resounded in my mind, "In order for people to start taking you serious, you have to first take yourself serious." It also reminded me of my father's words so long ago.

It was not that I was conditioned to believe a bogus, unidentifiable woman who was so chicken shit that she had to step to me over an email instead of in person, but James didn't give me much hope for our marriage to hold onto. Between his violent temper towards me, his unexplained time away from home, and his lies, I couldn't do anything but believe the message. It was funny how I knew the right thing to do, but either chose not to or was too afraid to put it in action.

From that moment, I planned to show James I was capable of living my life without abuse and infidelity. It started with that weekend away from home.

Throwing caution to the wind, I allowed the wind to move me closer to Miami. I did it for me. If only for a few days, I was living life to the fullest. It was funny how things worked themselves out. For the rest of my life, that weekend would often be remembered as the beginning of an era of loving me.

Chapter 8

Gladys

"If my cell phone rings again, I don't know what I'm going to do!" I received a couple calls from Rhonda that night before, back to back. I let them all go to voicemail. She cried and sounded upset on the messages, but figured she could talk to Shayla about her drama. If it was serious, Shayla would help her a lot faster than I could in Florida. To be honest, if it was some more drama about her family, her latest fling, or some other bull that I really didn't care about, I didn't want to listen to it while I was on my vacation.

The constant ringing of my phone jarred my mind back James, and everything I had going on at work. I wondered whether I faxed the last part of my firms' contractual agreement to Nordec University. We were slated to go live with Nordec, one of the largest facilities in the United States, and I was the consultant responsible for making it happen. The thought of not completing one detail was almost strong enough to make me want to turn around. The mere chance that I dropped the ball on any part of this deal made me cringe. A month ago, James lost his job, again. Therefore, he had time to ride my back about everything. This caused me to lose focus and possibly clients. Suddenly, my rising career was on the line with that Nordec account. I would sink or swim with the million-dollar client. If I swam, I would roll in pay dirt. If I sank, I would be in the unemployment line and hitting soup kitchens up within the blink of an eye.

Traffic was heavy as hell as I breezed down I-85. I dodged a truck that cut me off when my cell phone vibrated. Once I was secure in my lane, I checked the caller ID. It was James again. That time I answered. Skipping the formalities, I went straight to the point.

"I'm sorry, sweetheart, but I'm not coming back home. So, enjoy your time with the kids!"

He spat a few vulgar explicatives mixed with a threat. "I hope you enjoy your time away, because when you get back it's going to be trouble."

I sighed. Enjoying my newfound freedom, I said, "If you want to talk to me civil, we can talk. You are not going to holler at me or call me out of my name today. I will not accept it."

"You need to come back home," he said in a calmer voice.

"I'm not coming home." I, too, was cooler than a cucumber. Knowing he was hundreds of miles away and unable to strike was comforting.

My calmness unsettled him. He yelled all kinds of words into my ear and, had he caught me any other day, I would have been so fragile. I would have shattered under the intensity of his verbal assault. But, that day I had my own purpose and mission. “I’ll see you Monday, and we will talk then. Take care of my babies.” I told him. When those actual words slipped from my tongue, my stomach lurched at the thought of having to return Monday. I knew what awaited me there. I pressed visions of his fists to the back of my mind.

“What the hell has gotten into you, woman? You can’t just jump on the highway without discussing it with me! Oh, you just wait until I get my hands on you, you disrespectful bitch. You have no idea! I’m telling you to get your spic ass back home right now, and I mean now!”

I imagined him pacing the living room floor, furious. He probably punched holes in the walls once he realized nothing he said would change the way my wind blew. The winds of change pushed me toward Florida. I would not be waiting up for him until I was too tired to hold my eyes open. I cared less about how he felt about it.

"I am turning my cell phone off now," were my final words to him before I dropped the phone into my purse.

There was a time when his love awakened new things inside of me. The first time he put his hands on me that part of me perished. Yet, he kept right along living as if he didn’t recognize the corpse sleeping beside him. Perhaps he hadn’t.

It was time for my husband to get a taste of his own medicine. For too many years, I did not do anything that did not include him or the children. If it weren’t for my children, I would have ran away from our sorry excuse of a marriage years ago. Ever since we found out I was pregnant with Nazaria, it was my job to watch, protect, and provide for our children while he was a live-in deadbeat. For God's sakes, the man didn't even bring his paycheck home. And to think, I was only forcing him to be responsible for the kids for *one* weekend.

I didn't even confront him about the email from his trashy whore. Yet, I'd bet money that he had his mother on speed dial. You would think a woman would have sympathy towards her son's abused wife, but no. She wanted him to marry a black woman, so she turned a blind eye to my bruises.

Those two were the least of my worries as the hot Florida sunshine hit my face. I thought about my babies. My babies were awesome. I wouldn't change one thing about them – not even conceiving them with their ass clown of a father. As young as they were, they were all for me doing something that would make me happy.

I hated to admit it, but I was sure they knew their father hit me. I tried to keep them from it. I attempted to hide the bruises the best way possible, but they had a special sense for those types of things. They knew when mommy was hurting. I was sure they heard my cries in the middle of the night. At least, James did not show his hatefulness to them. They had his blood coursing through their veins, and that was precious to him.

Even with all that he did, I didn't step outside of our marriage. I believed if I was to do something, I had to do it with no regrets. That trip was the first step. I took a stand. My spirit was empowered. I smiled so big I thought the corners of my mouth were going to crack.

Yeah, sure, James was upset, but I was a woman on a mission. I took another look at the golden pass to spend three days and two nights at Fontainebleau Resort. I was anxious and excited about the masquerade party, my free hotel nights, and just the entire experience. I reached in my purse, pulled out my cell and turned it off.

"No more phone calls will interrupt my peace," I said.

Life sure wasn't the white picket fence, dinner and a movie that James promised, but a few relaxing days away from it all sounded better by the minute. I craved the peace and tranquility of the oceanfront. I threw caution to the wind. Turning up the volume on the radio, I erased all traces of home from my mind and pushed forward through the traffic.

Chapter 9

Shayla

Kicking off my shoes, I glanced at the half-carat diamond toe ring that accentuated my freshly manicured toes. As it shimmered under the dimmed recessed lighting, the milieu that surrounded me was breathtaking. I was a lucky woman. I had everything I could ever ask for, and more. I thanked God for His blessings.

Glancing at the clock, I was discouraged that it was 10:25 PM. I sat on the couch and wallowed in my sorrows. Usually, I accepted his lies and alibis. He would be MIA for a week and have the nerve to get mad if I asked where he had been and, by the time he got finished fussing and cussing, I felt like he put his hands all over me. I knew for a fact he was not above cheating. I'd caught him a time or two back when I was checking. With the quickness, he let me know he didn't appreciate me snooping around in his business.

The phone rang, breaking me away from my thoughts. It was Titus. I pressed END on his call and silenced the ringer. It was his time to sweat, just like I had done all day. A minute after the phone rang, the voicemail lit up indicating that he left a message. My stomach felt queasy; he was ready to feed me lies and I, like the fool I was, was ready to eat them with a smile.

I drifted to a place I'd rather be – in love. I imagined what it would be like to be married to a businessman who came home every evening, reached down to pet the dog, and kissed the kids on the forehead. I wondered what it would feel like to have a man who was attentive to his wife's needs, wants and desires. I could actually see myself falling in love with a man who thought finding a difficult word in a crossword puzzle was the highlight of the day. If that meant he was going to be home to whisper sweet nothings in my ear at the end of the night, I was all for it. That scenario was so foreign to me that it sounded like nothing but far-fetched fantasy.

It was a long day and I was tired. I had drifted to sleep dreaming about that businessman when the front door inched open. I slightly cracked my eyes open and saw my husband tiptoeing toward me with a dozen roses. Assuming I was asleep, he looked down at me on the couch and smiled. For a second or two, I could see a glimpse of regret slide across his face.

My auburn-colored hair was disheveled and hid my eyes. Titus didn't know I was watching his every move. He eased down onto one knee and gently pushed several strands of hair away from my face and neck, exposing my skin.

He'd once told me I was his 'Black Barbie.' As I lay on the couch admiring my husband admire me, I thought about that nickname. At that very moment, he had the same look of affection in his eyes he had when he first called me that.

I didn't give away the fact that I was in a fake slumber. I didn't so much as make one tiny movement, afraid I would ruin the tender moment. His eyes roamed over my body and he whispered, "Baby, you look like a goddess in your sleep. Mmmm. These silk pajamas are absolutely beautiful."

He retrieved a single rose from the dozen he placed on the coffee table, dangled the sweet flower near my face, and gently tickled my nose. When I didn't open my eyes, he gently shook my shoulder.

"Shayla? Wake up, babe."

I heard him come in, smelled the roses, felt his nudge, and heard him call my name, but I didn't make a move. If it was possible to be completely irritated and irreversibly in love with a person at the same time, that would explain how I felt.

He knelt down and kissed my cheek, lightly rubbing his fingers over my lips. "I'm sorry, babe," his bold voice spoke. "But, wake up. The night is still young."

Was that the best he could come up with? I thought. He was so selfish.

"Shayla. Come on, babe. I know you're up. You are not that good at faking. Daddy is sorry Mama," he said in the most humble voice he knew.

I rubbed my eyes and opened them. I looked at the clock and pointed at the time. It was 10:45 PM. I slowly sat up on the couch and stretched my arms to the sky as I took a nice, long yawn.

I said, "It's cute that you stroll in here with roses. It would have been cuter if you did it four hours ago."

He retrieved the other roses from the coffee table and held them out to me. "I am so sorry for missing dinner. It looks like you really laid it out, too."

I didn't accept the roses, so he placed them back on the coffee table. He put his hand on my chin to raise my eyes to meet his and I forced my face to turn away from him. "And I know you and Rhonda's secret," I admitted.

"What?" His jaw dropped open. "What do you mean?"

"Do you think I'm really that stupid?" I shouted. "After all, she is my best friend. She tells me everything."

"I... Baby... I..."

I eyed him suspiciously. "Yeah, I was stressed out and the whole time you were in Atlanta getting me a gift."

A look of confusion was on his face. "Atlanta?"

"She told me you were going to Atlanta to get me a present. Yet, you come home with these roses? The real gift must be in your pocket."

"Well, actually, I...was about to..."

I cut him off. "You mean to tell me you drove to Atlanta and all you came back with are some roses? That's the dumbest thing I ever heard in my life!"

I could have sworn I saw a slight smile cross his lips. He wiped his forehead and leaned in, "Shayla, baby... That was my fault. They didn't have your special ordered gift ready. You've got to let me make this up to you."

"I know you are not smiling," I said, thoroughly disgusted with his behavior. "How are you going to make it up to me? Do you think a new ring will work? Do you think you can just buy my happiness?"

"No. I don't think that."

"Well, if you don't love me, then why won't you just let me go?" I didn't quite plan that line of questioning. However, since the issues were on the table, I stared him straight in the eyes and waited on his answer.

"Listen, Shayla, I know you're upset, as you should be. I was wrong for standing you up, but you are the most important person in my life. This will *not* happen again."

"You do not love me. You only love your money and yourself."

"You are going overboard to even think I don't love you. I love you with everything I have in me, baby girl. Believe that."

He pressed his lips against mine and kissed me. Every two seconds, he broke the kiss to tell me how sorry he was. When he finally ended the kiss, he explained, "I had to set one of my suppliers straight tonight. From now on, you come first, Shayla. You."

Even though I knew I should stand my ground, his touch had an effect on me. I didn't know if what he said was a bunch of bullshit lies or if he was sorry for missing our date. Either way, if he thought coming in there with a simple explanation would suffice, he was wrong. I wanted to believe him. I really did. However, past experience taught me that everything was not as it seemed. I opened my mouth to give him a piece of my mind and realized he was unbuckling his pants. My husband's pants fell to the floor leaving him clad in a white white-beater and black boxer-briefs.

I rolled my eyes in an attempt to feed my anger. But, the pure sight of him took me to another place. I tried to think of Bible verses that would calm the matrimonial lust starting to take residence in my body. I needed anything that would allow me to be strong enough to tell him what was on my mind. However, a few things I could not deny: One, Titus was the finest piece of milk chocolate I ever had the pleasure of tasting. Two, I couldn't resist chocolate.

Two-hundred-and-ten-pounds of muscle stretched over a six-foot frame. Dreads neatly trimmed. Goatee trimmed perfectly across his jaw line. Flawlessly silky cocoa-brown skin. He possessed calf muscles so big and taut I would rub them for hours.

For the next minute, an internal struggle ensued. He *had* to pay for standing me up. As incredibly fine as he was, he got away with too much, too often. I bit my bottom lip and composed myself, so I could think of my next point of action.

Then, he put the icing on the cake and made my decision for me. He pulled me to my feet and our bodies meshed like they were meant to be one.

Involuntarily wrapping my arms around his neck, I closed my eyes and meditated for strength. "Titus, you are wrong," I whined.

His baritone whisper blew hot words into my ear. "Let me make it right."

The words maneuvered their way all through my body. I was hot from the inside out. He then pulled me back in for a long and tender kiss, moving his mouth from my lips to my neck, and finally traveling to my breasts. Realizing I was losing the battle with each passing moment, I digressed. I needed to feel the love he gave to me.

He searched my eyes to see. "Do you forgive me?"

Despite all common sense, I was ready to forgive. I stood there in a passionate stupor and said, "I forgive you. For now..."

Licking his lips in his signature LL style, he smiled. To break the awkward silence that followed, I giggled. The fact that he didn't make it home sooner was filed away in my mind, just like other broken promises, missed dates, and lonely nights.

"Come on," Titus said, as he secured me in his arms. He handled me effortlessly, making me feel as though I was as light as a feather. We kissed deeply as he walked the stairs two at a time, anxious to get to our bedroom.

Chapter 10

Titus

After making sweet love to my wife, I laid in bed enjoying the moment. I pulled the comforter over her so she wouldn't get cold. Laying in our bed, my wife had the afterglow of passion all over her beautiful skin. Watching her made me want to kick my own ass for even thinking about another woman. I had more than a man could ask for at home. What was I doing fucking her best friend? I shook my head. I was caught up.

I pushed Rhonda out of my mind. I didn't want to soil my bedroom with thoughts of her. I wrapped my arms tightly around wifey's waist and held her until sleep overtook me.

The next morning, I woke up to the smell of bacon, eggs, and fresh cinnamon. I hopped out of bed and dashed into the shower, so I could join Shayla in the kitchen. If I was lucky, I would get fresh cinnamon-flavored Shayla for breakfast, too. Once I dried off, I put on a pair of silk boxers and followed the aroma to the kitchen. I sprinted down the steps like a man that was born again.

When I entered the kitchen, I felt like vomiting in my throat. I lost my appetite when I saw Ronnie sitting across from my wife on the high-back breakfast chair in front of our French-style breakfast table.

The biggest grin was plastered on her face when she saw me. To my dismay, she beamed and pointed.

"Look who's out of bed, Shay! Good morning, sleepy head," she said.

I walked into the kitchen slowly and stood beside my wife's chair across from Rhonda. With an eye on Rhonda, I kissed Shayla on the cheek. "Yeah, I'm up," I said.

If she could read body language, she knew the next time I saw her alone I was going to administer a back hand slap to her crooked jaw on principal. She had some kind of nerve showing up there that morning.

"Hey, sleepy head," Shayla said, repeating Ronnie's words. Smiling as she spoke, my wife was perkier than ever. She had a way of lighting up a room. I wished I could appreciate her positive disposition fully, but Ronnie watching my every move made me salty.

"I thought you were going to sleep the day away, mister," Shayla said. She stood up, wrapped her arms around my neck, and kissed me. As I hugged and kissed my wife, I looked at Rhonda with fire in my eyes. I wished her ass would POOF and be gone.

When Shayla looked at me, she had an unmistakable look of pride on her face. She was happy to show our love in front of her friend. Little did she know, the woman sitting across the table was anything, but her friend.

"Guess what, baby?" she asked.

I looked at Ronnie and said, "Rhonda was just about to leave?"

"No, silly!" Shayla said. "I made your favorite omelet this morning. Bacon, ham and red peppers."

She walked over to the microwave and retrieved a saran-wrapped plate. A carefully prepared meal consisting of my favorite omelet, a half a dozen fresh sliced strawberries, and grits was perfectly arranged on my plate.

"I also made cinnamon waffles, but I was waiting for you to come down, so I could make yours fresh." Then, she whispered in my ear, "I planned to feed you breakfast in bed, but since Ronnie came over, we can just eat down here. She's feeling bad because some jerk she spent the night with last night attacked her."

I cringed as I took the plate out of Shayla's hand and said, "No need for you to make waffles now. I'll just take what you have ready upstairs and watch some ESPN. But, I want you back in bed ASAP woman."

I forced a smile and then turned my attention to our intruding guest, Rhonda.

"If you don't mind, the wife and I want to get back to bed, so don't keep her too long with your *issues*."

I put an emphasis on 'issues' to help her remember that her issues could get a whole hell of a lot worse.

"I will be up there soon, Titus Montre Wilson," Shayla said, twirling strands of hair around her finger.

Before turning to walk away, I gave Ronnie a silent threat warning her to hold her peace. Either she would heed that warning, or she would feel the burn of my piece.

Shayla followed behind me into the hallway. Speaking under her breath, she said, "Ronnie really needs us right now. A man jumped on her last night. "

Biting down on a piece of bacon, I said, "No shit?"

"Yeah, so give me just a few minutes to talk to her. She was just about to tell me who he was when you walked in, and if she tells me who this punk is, I want you to handle him. No man should put their hands on a woman."

My wheels turned. There was no way I could leave Shayla alone with Rhonda when she was threatening to drop the dime on us. I shook my head and said, "If you stay down here with her drama, you'll be down here until night falls. I tell you what. You mosey them fine ass hips of yours on upstairs and get ready for a double dose of last night, and I'll get the rest of the story, including the name of this punk from Rhonda."

"Aw, you would help her like that?"

"I put my life on the fact that she won't have to worry about that happening to her again! I got this." I had to take control of this situation and fast.

Shayla stood there for a second or two thinking about my offer. "Maybe we should talk to her together," she said.

"We both know she's a drama queen. If you talk to her, she'll talk, whine and gossip all day. If I talk to her, I'll get straight to the point. I will talk to her from a man's perspective of what she should do, find out who it is, and handle him."

She was reluctant, but she said, "Okay, I'll let you handle it."

"Good. I know she needs your help, but we need this time together. It's been so long that we have had personal time together. I don't want to waste our time dealing with other people's problems, so go on up to the bedroom and I'll be up there in a few minutes."

After I laid it out there, Shayla finally submitted. "Thanks for being there for my sister. No one has the right to treat her like that."

"Don't you worry your pretty little head. I got this," were my final words before Shayla went back into the kitchen.

"Rhonda," she said. "I want you to tell Titus what happened and then we have some things to do, so he will let you out. Don't worry. He's going to make sure that guy does not come back around bothering you. I'm going upstairs and will call you later this evening."

Ronnie looked as if she'd hit pay dirt. "Okay, Shay," she said.

I watched Shayla climb the stairway. Once she was at the top of the stairs, she closed the bedroom door behind her. Sweat beaded on my forehead as I walked into the kitchen. I wasn't even the type of nigga to break a sweat, normally. But, Rhonda darkening my doorstep with that bullshit made me madder than a motherfucking bulldog on red meat. What kind of game was she trying to play with a nigga like Tee? Man, she was a glutton for punishment; she was about to get checkmated.

Rhonda sat near the island and, when I walked into the kitchen, her eyes popped wide open with surprise.

"Where is Shayla?" she asked when she didn't see her with me.

"Get yo' motherfucking ass the hell out of my house, woman! You know good and well I'm not about to stand by and let you tell Shayla about us. You are testing me for the second time in twenty-four hours. What, you didn't get enough last night?"

"Hold on a minute now, big boy. I didn't mention your name. But, I knew coming here would get your attention. I just wanted you to know that I'm still here and not going anywhere. All I want is your attention."

Her cocky ass got up from her seat, walked over, stood directly in front of me, and puckered her lips for a kiss.

I shoved her away. "What the fuck is your problem? Are you fuckin' crazy, Rhonda?"

"Only about you."

I grabbed her arm, walked her toward the front door, and opened it. "Look, you crazy bitch... I told you this 'me and you' thing is a figment of your imagination. The only couple up in here is me and my wife that just walked up those steps." Through tightly pursed lips, I said, "Now get out of my house!"

She refused to walk through the door. She closed it and searched my face for answers. "Titus... Tee... I really think you need to think about this, baby. You don't want me to start singing like a canary, do you? If you keep treating me like a piece of gum on the bottom of your shoes, you will feel my wrath. And Tee? Trust me; *I* don't even know how far I will go to hit back. You don't want it to go there and neither do I. You wanted to try me out, and you tried it. Now, you've got me... until death do we part!"

Her grin was insane but, for some awkward reason, I liked it. Her hand gently inched down until it reached and stroked my manhood.

"Go'n with that bull, Rhonda." I shifted my weight onto my right foot and pushed her away, again.

"Hell, you've been getting this for years and now you want to act like you're husband of the year?" She touched me again and kissed my neck. "Oh, no. We are connected. I know what you want."

Her touch was like water. It doused the flame of my anger. I allowed Ronnie to touch me for far too long and, before I knew anything, she stroked me straight into stupid. I called it the stroke of lust. I should have thrown her out of my house on her face. But, with a stroke of lust, I allowed her to seduce me at my front door. I let out several deep breaths and licked my lips as she slid her palm up and down my shaft. The adrenaline and testosterone pumping through my veins betrayed me as nut filled my boxers.

"I'm not going anywhere. And from the looks of things, you don't want me to," she said with a soft chuckle. She touched her lips with her hand covered in my seed and licked her fingers.

I stared at her, bracing myself against the wall beside the door. My knees were weak and, apparently, so had my mind.

She placed her free hand on my chest. Every inch of my body was sensitive. Ronnie was ruthless in her pursuit, which was what made her so damn sexy to me in the first place.

Since I gave her the upper hand (literally), again, I asked her to leave nicely. My willpower was low, but she had to get the hell out of there before Shayla came downstairs. If she came down right then, she would know what had happened; she knew how I looked after I busted a good nut.

I could hear the shower running upstairs and Shayla singing to her own beat. She was unaware that treachery in its highest form was taking place in her living room. The truth was that I wanted my wife – and I wanted Ronnie.

"Just leave, baby, and we'll hook up later tonight. I promise," I told her as I opened the door again.

Instead of honoring my request, Rhonda pushed the door closed, took me by the hand, and led me into the den. My mind screamed for me to man up and throw her out of the house like an old piece of furniture, but my body didn't protest.

"Ronnie, you need to go ahead and leave. I'm not doing anything else with you in my house." I sounded desperate asking her to leave. How had I lost control that fast? I sounded like a punk begging her to leave my house before I fucked the shit out of her with my wife upstairs. My words didn't match my actions, so she ignored my weak ass protest. Hell, I would have ignored it too. After all, I did follow her into the den like a blind sheep, and Big Tee was standing up straight against my belly like a baseball bat.

She purred, as she closed the den door and locked it. "You called me Ronnie, which means you want me. I know you too good."

She did know me. When a woman knew your weakness, the game is over. Behind the den's locked door, she pushed me up against the wall and released my throbbing manhood from my boxers. She dropped to her knees shamelessly and began sucking me so good that I was powerless to put up much of a fight.

"This is fucked up," was the only comment I made as I grabbed the back of her head and pushed my dick further down her throat. What we were doing was wrong. It was also the type of cheap thrill that most men would give their left arm for. It was the reason I fucked her in the first place.

Her hand tightened around my shaft as her lips, tongue, and throat continued the job of pleasuring me once again. Removing my dick from her dripping wet mouth, she said, "You love it though."

I was clocked out for at least a full five minutes. When my hot cum released into her throat, I was spent. "Oh, Ronnie... Make Big Tee cum. That's right, get back in good with Daddy."

The den had a lock on the door and a side exit door. Once her scheme was complete, she picked up her purse off the floor and disappeared out the door without speaking another word. I leaned against the door for a few seconds before remembering my situation. Shaking my head at the love triangle I was tangled in, I went into the kitchen and warmed up the breakfast food.

"What's taking you so long, baby?" Shayla yelled, standing at the top of the stairs in her pink negligee.

I took a deep breath. "Uh... Just getting some wine for you, Shay. I'll be there in a minute."

Was I really ready to face my wife? I guessed I had to be. I took a paper towel from the holder, wiped the sweat from my forehead, retrieved two wine glasses from the cellar, and trotted toward the steps. That shit Ronnie did was too close for comfort. I was a dog, but I loved my wife. I had to get that situation under control... and soon.

Chapter 11

Shayla

Long Time Coming

I showered, applied lotion, and put on a delectable two-piece lingerie set. Titus, still had not made it back up to our bedroom to eat his breakfast. I smiled as I thought back to the time when he hired Chef Balal to prepare a romantic dinner serenaded by the famous singer Joe in the comfort of our dining room, I knew he was a special man when he wanted to be.

I snapped back from that sentimental trip down memory lane and peaked out the bedroom door. Rhonda must had talked Titus's head off by then, I reasoned. I hoped he got the name and address of the punk that abused her. I could not stand men who were abusive.

I called out to him. "Titus?" The house was quiet.

He didn't answer, so I thought that Ronnie must have left. I slowly descended the staircase making sure not to make a sound. I had a surprise or two for Titus that I knew he would enjoy. Moving like a model on the runway, I tiptoed through the living room. The edible gold-toned lotion spread over my body was ready to be licked, bitten, eaten and kissed. Edible nipple pastries and panties were about to make for a full course meal for my husband. When he had his fill, I planned to take him into the shower and break in the new shower rod. The toils of a freaky housewife were never done.

For a few fleeting seconds, I felt like the silly little girl who fell in love with him on the schoolyard. To keep that feeling alive, I was willing to give the best of me to a man who would no doubt take, and in a few days he would go back to being a part-time husband. I pushed those irritating thoughts to the back of my mind, unwilling to let reality ruin rare moments of happiness. I decided a long time ago to take the good with the bad. I knew the role of a "kept woman." Even though he married me, I was still stowed away like a mistress. I enjoyed the glitz and glam of being the first woman to a made man and made the best of the time we had together.

I searched the kitchen with no luck. As I walked out of the kitchen and approached the den, the sounds of sensual moans resonated through the door. I knew he was not in there watching porn when I was waiting on him. "I must have left that TV on earlier," I said, as I reached for the door handle.

Just as quickly as I reached for the handle, I released it, like it was hot fire. When I heard my best friend's distinctive voice say, "You love it though." My brow wrinkled up in a confused scowl. I felt my nostrils begin to flare as I pursed my lips together to suppress the shout of surprise that threatened to come forth.

Then, my husband let out a moan and replied, "Oh, Ronnie... Make Big Tee cum. That's right, get back in good with Daddy."

Hearing Titus say that to another female was inconceivable. I had to be hearing things. Surely, my husband and my best friend were not getting it on, in my den, while I listened on the other side of the door. I pressed my ear against the mahogany wood and heard unmistakable sounds of moaning and dirty talk. Disturbing thoughts flashed through my mind.

I saw Rhonda's smiling face staring at me that morning as I explained to her how Titus came home late the night before. I remembered describing our feverish love making, and how silent she sat while I told her the intimate details. Titus' shocked face when he saw Rhonda sitting in our kitchen and how he insisted he help her, while I waited like a dumbass upstairs, flashed before my eyes. I was unable to feel or think coherently. Every emotion seemed to push itself into my head at the same time, and none of them were good.

When I pressed my ear firmly against the door a second time and heard my husband's moans, along with slurping and sucking sounds, hurt overrode all other feelings. It flowed through me like a rushing river. If what I imagined was happening, my heart was broke in two directions.

"Titus, you like that? I told you Shayla can't do you like I can," caused my stomach to begin to hurt as much as my spirit, tying itself up into a million tightening knots. I just could not believe my ears. There was no turning back. It was happening, and it was happening in my home. My beautiful... expensive... expertly designed... house of lies.

I was frozen in place, unable to run from the incomprehensible situation, but unable to stay. After the night we shared together, after getting up and cooking him breakfast, and after preparing to spend another beautiful day with him, I realized it meant nothing. I shuddered under the weight of anger and disrespect I felt. Why hadn't I listened to mama all those times she told me, "Never tell your friends your personal business about you and your man. They act like they care about you, but they listening. They listening too hard," mama had said. That conniving bitch allowed me to pour my heart out to her so many times. I fought the urge to burst through the door and put that whore's weave straight through my plasma television.

I took two steps away from the doorknob as if it turned into a four-eyed monster. At the moment, I was unsure of any of the people that were supposed to be close to me. Everything I believed in changed. I could have been bought and sold for a quarter. That's how cheap I felt. I was played like a twenty-five-cent video game, and they both had the controllers. I didn't know what to do, so I did what came natural to me. I ran. With no place to go, I ran back up to my bedroom.

As I sank down into the bed, reality fell on my shoulders like a ton of bricks. My best friend was my husband's mistress. While I cried on her shoulder, taking her advice and appreciating her attentiveness, she stabbed me in the back with the precision of a surgeon. She was careful to keep me alive, but injured nonetheless. With that incision, they went for blood. I was cut deep.

"No!" I screamed into a pillow. I wondered how long they had been slithering around on their bellies like the snakes that they were. "How could Ronnie do this to me? I've loved her since we were kids!"

When Rhonda was sixteen, her mother kicked her out the house. Her stepfather didn't want her there, so I convinced Mama to let Rhonda move in with us. She was like the sister I never had. I shared everything with her from that day on. Apparently, we were still sharing, more than I knew. Eventually, Rhonda's mother chose her husband over her and never allowed her to come back home.

I looked at Rhonda's picture that sat in a frame on my dresser and tried to imagine why she would hit me so low. If she thought she was going to ride of into the sunset with my husband, she had another thing coming.

"Ugh! I can't believe her! I guess she thinks screwing my husband is worth losing a sister for life. If she thinks for one minute I'm going to sit around and watch her ride off into the sunset with my husband, she has the whole situation messed up. I will leave him on my own terms, not hers or his!" I screamed into my pillow.

I had loved them both. They apparently did not share the same love for me. After spending a few agonizing minutes in prayer, the uncontrollable anger that attempted to overtake me gave way to tears that flowed freely for the next few minutes. Feeling as though I were having an out of body experience, I found the strength to rise. I went into the bathroom, freshened up and, with only God holding me up, I managed to pull myself back together.

For the first time in our married life, I felt detached from my own feelings. Standing at the top of the stairs in my pink negligee, I steadied my voice, and called out, "Titus, what's taking you so long, baby?"

He said, "Uh. Just getting us some wine for you, Shay. I'll be there in a minute."

"Sure," I said, as I walked back into my room and sat on the bed. As I waited for my husband, it felt good to be in control, for once. He and his wench weren't calling the shots anymore.

The famous poet, William Blake, said it best – "in love, there is a smile of love and there is a smile of deceit. Then there is the smile of smiles in which those two smiles meet."

That was the day I met the beautifully ugly smile of deceit.

Chapter 12

Gladys

Eventually, I arrived in Fontainebleau's lobby. Unlike the tense drive over, I felt like a runaway slave that made it to the North. I was stress free, work free, husband free, and childfree. Simply free. The fresh air that filled my lungs seemed to move in and out more freely. I fought off any feeling of guilt for the stolen free time. "I needed this," I said to no one in particular.

After ten minutes of waiting in the long reception line, I checked into my room and headed to my suite. The bellhop, who so graciously brought my belongings up to my room, told me some great site seeing locations. I tipped him and then unpacked my bags. I placed each outfit on a hanger and put the undergarments inside of the dressers.

My plan was to get dressed and then go down to the bar to see if any of my old classmates were hanging out. When I moved to Valley, I lost contact with just about everyone from college. I was anxious to see my old friends. I showered with White Diamonds body wash, dried off, and applied a generous amount of lotion to my skin. I chose a form-fitting black shirt and black tights with an oversized black belt. Stiletto heels added a nice touch to my outfit. When I released my shoulder length blond-streaked hair from the bow I wore, it hung beautifully in an array of fluffy curls around my neck.

With pure confidence, I headed to the bar and grille, looking and feeling like a million bucks. That feeling was short lived, because I felt as tall as an ant when a familiar face caught my eye. Sitting at a corner table was Maverick Douglas.

He was easy on the eyes, gorgeous even. His smile could melt an ice sculpture. Back at Albany State in Georgia, I was madly in love with Maverick. Every moment I spent with him was precious. I memorized the smooth terrain of his body and his amazing eyes. His coarse goatee tickled my stomach when he kissed my belly before we made love. Chestnut brown skin covered his tall and slender frame that melded into my flesh whenever we became one.

However, our relationship was far more than romance. His intelligence was just as intriguing. I was free to be myself with him. In his arms, there was comfort and security. I rested in him. Does that make sense? I *rested* in him. Underneath the shade of campus trees, we talked for hours about current events and our studies. We discussed opinions about major political issues. We talked about family. We talked about love. He felt like *home.* I knew when we each got our degrees, we would be happily ever after. Buy the perfect home, get the perfect dog, and have a house full of perfect children. That was the plan, until he lost interest in me.

There were days he didn't call. He said he was studying for engineering classes and didn't have time. Our once inseparable relationship was reduced to moments in passing. We took the role of two class friends, instead of the lovers we were meant to be. Convinced he had another girlfriend, I was jealous. I pictured what she looked like. How she walked, laughed at his jokes, and stroked his hair. I tortured myself with these thoughts. He tried to assure me his schedule was full, and that he was busy, but jealousy led to me breaking off the relationship. I remember that evening vividly. I called him just before summer break. It was a call I would live to regret.

"There's my Honey Love," he answers on the third ring.

"I'm glad you decided to answer." I speak a mile a minute. I want to get my thoughts out before I lose the nerve to say what I feel. I am stern and get straight to the point. "It's obvious you don't have any time for me, so instead of being strung along longer than necessary, I think it's best that we just split up now."

"Gladys, I've been studying for finals."

I can't stand to listen to a lie, so I stop him before he tells one. "No. Don't say anything. I'm doing what's in our best interest, Maverick, so let's cut our losses early. This way you are free to do your thing, and I'm free to do mine."

"Honey Love..."

Honey Love is a nickname he gave to me when we first started dating. I am not trying to be lovey-dovey, so I want him to stop with the pet names.

"Listen, I'm woman enough to tell you how I feel. Take care of yourself, Maverick." I hang up the phone and cry like a baby.

That summer, I went home to my parents and did not hear from Maverick. When the fall session began, I found out he didn't enroll at Albany. His brother told me he was accepted to an engineering program in another state. Just like that, he vanished from my life without a trace. My senior year, I met James at a fraternity party. We hit it off, and it wasn't long before we were at the altar.

Looking in Maverick's direction at the bar, my internal voice whispered calm words to my spirit. I had to maintain my composure. I wanted to ask him a million questions and catch up with what was going on in his life. I wondered if he was married. Did he have a little Maverick Jr. at home – or maybe two or three? Did he become an engineer (I had no doubt that he had). Where did he live? As much as I wanted to find out those things about him, I kept my distance. I didn't want to have to answer questions about my life.

Had I reacted prematurely when I had broke things off with him? When I was young and muy estupido, I hadn't thought out the consequences of my actions. Yet, deep down, I always knew we'd see each other again. Then, when the opportunity to touch him in the flesh was right in my face, I stood there frozen in time. I began to hyperventilate, so I quickly flagged the bartender down for a drink.

"Yes ma'am, what would you like?"the bartender asked.

I needed a few martinis to face an inevitable meeting with my past. "Extra strong cotton candy martini, please," I said. My mind moved a mile a minute. Did Maverick know I would be at the ball? Did he see me when I walked in, but ignore me? If I approached him, what would he say? Does he hate me? What if he hates me? What if he doesn't? What if he wraps his arms around me and asks me to go to his room?

I had so many questions. O, Dios mio, it was only by the grace of God that I kept my composure. Finally, my drink arrived, and I took a long swig of the heavenly fluid. Within minutes, the numbing effect gave me the nerve to take another glance in Maverick's direction. Just like before, he'd vanished. I didn't know whether to be disappointed or relieved that he was gone. The whole sighting was probably my mind playing tricks on me, anyhow – nothing but wishful thinking on my part. I continued to nurse my drink. Then, without warning, two words I had not heard in years sent a raging heat from the top of my head down to the tips of my toes.

Chapter 13

Gladys

"Honey Love?" he said. The warmth from the baritone whisper against my ear warmed my entire soul from the inside out.

I sat in my seat trapped in a moment of time. I yearned for that moment to transform into years earlier when those two words meant safety and security. I was frozen as the familiar smell of mahogany overtook my senses. I didn't want to turn around and face the owner of that sensual whisper and delightful warmth. To look into the eyes of the owner of that voice would send me to a place detrimental to my livelihood, as I knew it.

"You're still as beautiful as you were the last day I laid eyes on you," he said with his customary sultry swagger. He placed his right hand on the small of my back and gently massaged the tension building there.

I knew my face had to be perfectly rosy from surprise. That man – the man blowing his alcohol-tinged breath into my right ear – I had loved for years, even in his absence. Especially in his absence.

"Maverick?" I took a long breath and slowly turned to face my past lover. He was stunningly handsome. I was taken aback by how much changed, for the better. Once tall and slender, he was tall with stout muscular shoulders. He looked like he could walk on as a starter for a NFL football team. As I surveyed every inch of his body, one thought crossed my mind. He was sexy.

Oblivious that he was affecting me, his full and sumptuous lips began to move. He probably spoke words I needed to hear in order to hold a normal reunion conversation, but I was tone deaf at that moment. I took in another sip of my drink and glanced over the body of the man I once called mine. Leisurely dressed in a blue buttoned-down shirt, blue jeans and white tennis shoes, he would look fabulous in anything.

As I nervously held onto my drink, I imagined the mounds of beautiful skin underneath his clothes. Before I knew anything, the drink was completely gone. The loud gurgling sound from my straw snapped me back into reality. It was then that I finally heard the words coming out of his mouth.

"Dang girl, I'll buy you another drink. You don't have to slurp that one until all the bubbles are gone out of the glass." His dimples sank on either side of his chiseled face as he spoke.

"Oh, my bad." I could have melted into the floor. I made a fool of myself and couldn't help it. The man was fine.

He let out a loud chuckle and I couldn't help but join in. Memories of his tender touch flooded my mind. My heart never forgot how much I loved him.

Then my mind went there. There was no way a qualified chica had not snatched him up. He had 'TAKEN' written all over him. I didn't want to go there, but I did. *Maybe it's the same woman he cheated on me with in college,* I somberly thought.

A vision of the woman I dreamt of found itself in my mind. I pictured her to be an Asian woman with long jet-black hair down to her waist. Maverick had spoken a few times about wanting to study abroad in Asia, and I could just see him with an oriental woman on his arm.

"I'm sorry, Maverick. You really caught me by surprise. Seeing you after all of this time, let's just say it's overwhelming," I told him.

He took a step closer to me, tucked a stray curl behind my ear and said, "When I saw you sitting over here, I thought my mind was playing tricks on me. I was beginning to think I would never see you again."

The words he spoke were completely innocent, but the simmer in his eyes spoke in volumes. Volumes I was in no way prepared to handle. The way he said "...beginning to think I would never see you again," sounded to me like he'd wanted to see me again. I tried not to read too much into his statement. After all, I was a married woman.

Attempting to turn the heat down a notch, I said, "Well, here we are. What kind of business are you in town for?"

"I live in Miami now," he said, taking a seat in the empty barstool beside me.

"Wow! What is the chance that the two of us would end up in Miami, at the same hotel, on the same weekend?"

"I come to this bar quite often. They have the best bourbon chicken wings in town. But, if you remember correctly, then you already know my theory on chance." He nonchalantly smiled and shrugged his shoulders.

"Nothing in life happens by chance. Everything we encounter has purpose," I said, and had a quick impulse to grab for my new drink. He caught my hand before I could do so.

"Exactly," he said, looking deeply into my eyes as if he was searching for something he left there. He paused for a moment allowing his theory to take its full effect on me. "You remembered."

"Yes, what did you think I would forget?"

Instead of answering, he smiled and changed the subject with a compliment. "You are looking good. How has life been treating you?"

I definitely didn't want to think about my life and how it had been treating me, so I shrugged my shoulders and gave a typical answer. "I've been okay, and you?"

Blush rushed across my cheeks as his hand covered mine on the countertop. His fingers moved gently over my wedding band.

"Just okay, Marisol? You always deserve better than 'okay.' I hope you are not settling for that now. You are an amazing woman."

I sat silent. Settling for okay was something Maverick didn't believe in. But, that was back in college when we were young and naïve. It was a new day where grown up responsibilities, travesties, and reality set in. The real world was not fantasy and lights. When I found my voice, I conjured up the enthusiasm to tell a convincing lie.

"No, actually, life is great, Maverick," I said, nodding my head. I switched the conversation to a bright spot. "I have two beautiful kids that keep me busy every day, a two-year-old daughter and a four-year-old son. Their names are Nazaria and Kelvin."

"Really?" he said. If I didn't know any better, I would have thought a tinge of disappointment settled on his face.

"Yes. They are the reason that I wake up every morning and the reason I work as hard as I do. They keep me going." I nudged his strong shoulder, and asked, "Okay, how about you and yours? Tell me all about them."

"What about me and mine?" Maverick asked.

I gently nudged his shoulder, again. I knew there had to be a model tucked away somewhere. Maverick Douglas was not curling up at night alone.

"Don't play coy, Mr. Still-Fine-As-Hell. Who is the lucky lady?"

Anticipating his answer, I picked up my drink and took another long swig.

"I don't have a lucky lady," he said. "Still looking for that special someone to share my life with, ya know?"

"You don't have to lie to me. Surely, someone has snagged you up by now. There is no way you should be single."

"There were many women who tried to 'snag' me. I just haven't found the right one. I'm not willing to settle for just 'okay.' I'm searching for the extraordinary. In order for me to make anyone my wife, she is going to have to take my breath away just at the mere sight of her." Once again, he covered my hand with his.

"There was this one girl that I was in love with once. Since being with her, I've never found another girl to compare. Unfortunately, I made a mistake when I had her. I was working so hard to make something out of my life – so that I could have something to give her. I never got to show her how much I loved her. Since her, I haven't been able to love anyone else quite the same. Now, *she* was the one – a woman that will always be special to me. If I had *her* by my side, I would be complete. I guess I've been waiting on the time that we would meet again, and I was hoping that if the stars were aligned just right when that meeting occurred, I'd have another chance at love."

The depth of Maverick's words touched me so deeply. I wished I was the woman he spoke so affectionately about. If he felt that way about me eight years ago, we wouldn't have been sitting there having that conversation. I would be Gladys Marisol Douglas with a house full of little amazing Douglas children. I would have gone to the end of the earth for that man. Listening to him profess his undying love for that woman who had broken his heart was more than I could bear.

"I know losing that woman was hard on you. I know the kind of loss you are talking about, all too well."

I tossed back the rest of my drink and slipped down from the barstool. Our once intertwined hands gently slid apart.

"I have an event in a few hours, so I guess this is goodbye," I said. I didn't have an anywhere to go, but I had to get away before any more raw emotions overtook me. Hearing him talk about that woman was more than I could bear. I planted a kiss on his cheek, and my lips lingered a few seconds longer than cordial. "Take care of yourself, Mav."

"You too, Marisol," he said softly.

I made a hasty getaway, careful not to look back.

Chapter 14

Shayla

Titus made a point to stay at home the rest of the evening. He wined and he dined me as if he had not just gotten down and dirty with Rhonda in our den. I managed to divide my mind and heart from my body when he wanted to have sex. I was impressed with my ability to hide my true feelings. We were lying in bed after another round of amazing sex, when he rolled over and placed an arm around me. A prideful grin covered his face.

"Shayla, I called The Pampering Queen over, so you have a manicure and pedicure appointment at three."

"Oh, really? She just came over yesterday. Don't my toes look fabulous?" I stretched my leg out until my toes were inside of his mouth.

"Baby, everything about you is fabulous!" he said, before sucking my big toe. "Don't worry, I'll cancel it, then."

Suck my foot, you dog! I thought as I watched him suck my toe in and out of his mouth. My thoughts were vengeful, but the sweet smile on my face hid the venom.

Later, I found out that he also planned a surprise trip to New York to attend a Beyonce' concert that night. Guilt must had been eating at him to do so many sentimental things in one day. Days ago, I would have been on cloud nine traveling with my gorgeous husband. But, that day I wanted to kill him.

I accepted the invitation to New York. Hell, who was I to miss an opportunity to see Bey. I didn't let his indiscretions cause me to miss out on that great opportunity. Once we arrived, he asked me to take a walk in the park. Madison Square Park was a nice change of scenery from the countryside of Georgia. I took in every bustling minute of the fast city. We walked and talked as if we were getting to know each other all over again. I didn't give him any inkling that I was aware of his affair with Rhonda.

That night we relaxed in each other's arms until the early morning hours. We were in a five-star hotel close to the airport. When we returned home on Sunday evening, Titus didn't so much as check his cell phone. He didn't call his boys over to hang out. I soaked up every moment of my husband's time that he had to offer. For the first time in a very long time, he was all about us. It felt good to be together, but it was too little – too late. Sooner or later, I had to deal with the elephant in the room – his affair with Rhonda.

"Do you *have* to go to California tomorrow?" I asked him. He was in the closet packing a suitcase. He was hyped about getting to California to 'straighten out an employee.'

"I wish I didn't have to go, but I gotta take care of this messed up money situation. Fa Ya Grillz has an accounting issue that I got to straighten out personally. Niggas get out of line when the big dog is away, so I have to put my feet on the ground on this one."

"Okay, then," I said.

He kissed my forehead. "It shouldn't take more than a day or two to get this straight. Then I'll be on the first thing smoking back to my baby." He planted a kiss on my forehead and placed garments into his suitcase. After a few moments, he realized I was still standing there, visibly upset. He thought it was about that trip, but I had so much on my mind. He wrapped his arms around me. His hands slithered like snakes down my back to my hips.

"What? My baby wants some time with Big Tee before I go? Is that what you need, baby?"

Make Big Tee cum for me, Ronnie, my mind flashed back as he lustfully kissed me and his hands traveled all over my body. I immediately pictured him with Rhonda in the same way. For all I knew, he was headed to her house for the next few days.

"No!" I pushed him away hard. "I do not 'want some time' before you go. We need to work on our marriage. I'm coming with you," I stated matter-of-factly.

There would be no more begging, asking, hoping, and wishing for things I wanted. There would be demands. I was going to be the one telling him what was going to happen – not the other way around. Thank God, my alarm went off. No more snooze buttons and there would be no more sleeping with my eyes open.

When a man buried a woman up to her neck in stress and hurt, he didn't have one problem shoveling a couple more inches of shit on top of her. I was not going to stand around and let Titus shovel any more of his shit in my direction. I was either going to be his Queen, or the thorn in his side.

I felt my spine thicken. I didn't know if I should thank Rhonda for jarring me out of my stupor, or kick her ass for crossing the invisible line in the sand.

Clearly shocked and thoroughly irritated, Titus hands were suspended in air. When he realized I wasn't joking, he tried to play me to the left. "I'm handling business! You know you can't come with me. Get me that blue shirt out the dresser, aight?" He turned and walked away.

"No."

"Shay, I said, get me that blue shirt. Quit playin', girl. Don't ruin a good day, okay?"

"I said… I'm…. coming… with … you." I said it slow, in case he didn't hear me the first time.

There was an awkward moment that passed between us as Titus stared at me. He smiled and turned on his charm.

"I don't think that is a good idea. Things might get crazy out there, and my first duty is to protect you, my Queen. I can't let anything happen to you. You stay here, and I'll be back in a few days and then we can take a trip to wherever you want to go."

Ignoring his tired attempt at ditching me, I grabbed my suitcase and said, "I'm tired of the bullshit! I said I'm going, and that's final."

To my surprise, he caved and said, "Get packed then. But, you're gonna have to stay in the background. I don't want any of those niggas out west to know you are with me. There is no telling what kind of move they will try to make."

As I packed my clothing into my leather travel bag, I felt more like a woman than I had my entire life. If I'd known that putting my foot down was so much more gratifying than wallowing in sorrow, I would have done it a long time ago. I had at feeling growing in my gut that things were about to change for the better.

Chapter 15

Gladys

As I entered the masquerade ball Saturday night, the scene was something out of an exotic fairytale. The room was lit by red candles on the counters, tables, and booths. It had the fixings for a naughty getaway. Lovers cuddled, laughed, and caressed each other. Their faces glowed. Red streamers and white lights draped the ceiling. A sultry slow jam mesmerized bodies that moved to the rhythm of the beat. I inhaled the ambience and took it all in.

I wished James and I shared moments like that. He used to take me dancing Friday nights and we'd have candle lit dinner. Where had the love gone? The silky, red mask I wore had black striations and two red feathers on each side. It was a cute addition to my sleek V-neck black dress and accessories by Kimora Simmons. My hair fell around my shoulders in a cascade of curls. I felt like Beyonce didn't have anything on me!

I mixed and mingled a little bit and spotted an old friend, Gloria Dennis. Walking in her direction, I caught a glimpse of a masked male dancer. He removed his clothes as he gyrated his body sensuously to the music. Standing in a cage, he wore a pair of tight leather pants and a facemask. He had my undivided attention when he did a handstand and full split mid-air. I submitted to the hypnotic trance of his movements and it felt good! I danced to the beat.

"Brenda knows how to throw a party!" I said, so caught up looking at the dancer that I forgot about Gloria.

A whole lot of years and a month of Sundays had passed since I was out on the party scene like that without James. That type of atmosphere was a setting for guilty pleasures. I needed a cigarette.

"Martini on the rocks, please," I told the bartender once I worked my way to the bar.

I looked around and that time didn't see Gloria due to the masks covering most of the guests' faces. If Brenda were to walk past me, she wouldn't have known who I was and vice versa. An hour and three martinis later, I was really feeling the vibe. Moving from the bar to an empty booth close to the dance floor, I had the perfect spot for viewing the dancers in various cages throughout the room.

I picked up my glass to take another swig of my drink and the hairs stood up on arms, as if a draft came through the room. I sensed him before he spoke.

His lips grazed my earlobe as he leaned down and spoke. "What's a pretty lady like you doing sitting alone?" His baritone caused my lips to turn up into the biggest smile. I felt his body slide into the seat against me. To say I was on fire would have been an understatement. In attempt to diffuse that fire, I took that huge gulp of my drink and slid over in the booth.

Like déjà vu, the masked gentleman intertwined his fingers with mine. His mask was black with red stripes and though his identity was meant to be somewhat of a mystery, the familiar physique he so beautifully possessed was prominent through the midnight black suit.

"Mav..." I couldn't even get the rest of his name out. My mind and body responded to his touch – sweaty palms, dreamy eyes, and aching in my soul to kiss, hug, and touch him all over. Instead of acting out my thoughts or acknowledging the fact we were sitting hand in hand staring deeply into each other's eyes, I simply said, "So, I see red is still your favorite color."

He dressed like a refined, distinguished gentleman, which was undeniably a turn on. Every second he sat next to me staring through his mask was evident that the alcohol was working against my battle to maintain my composure.

"Red is *our* color, remember?" He said, removing his hand from mine long enough to tug the red mask covering my eyes.

"I remember the matching red knit sweaters we wore in the winter. We were so corny."

A deep-set genuineness was in his voice when he said, "I don't think we were corny. I think we were in sync with each other's style, Marisol."

He was the only person in the world that called me by my middle name and as it rolled off his tongue, I turned away and pretended to be engrossed in R. Kelly's song, *Feelin' On Your Booty.* The song was a fun selection, but it could get things started on a whole other level. Back in the day, we used to get down to every last one of R. Kelly's songs.

As if he knew what I was thinking, he stood, took me by the hand, and guided me to the dance floor. I followed his lead without hesitation. The pulsating lyrics vibrated through the speakers and facilitated our movement. *This is my song. For real, no doubt. Said the DJ is making me feel thugged out. As I walk you to the dance floor, we begin to dance slow. Put your arms around me. I'm feeling on your...*

"Boo-oo-ootie!" Maverick haphazardly sang along, mocking R. Kelly. His hands moved lower than they should've been. His body glided against mine.

I didn't care how silly he sounded. I closed my eyes and rested my head on the nape of his neck. I was going, going... almost gone to that place. A place romantically and passionately every woman should go at least once in a lifetime.

Once Maverick stopped singing, he squeezed me tightly in his arms. I made a move that even I didn't comprehend. I laid everything on the line.

"Will you spend the night with me tonight?" I asked. My husband had stolen my esteem and, in that question, I pled with Maverick to help it return.

He placed a soft kiss on my lips and said, "I planned to."

With that said, I melted into his arms with no thought of my life at home waiting for me. I was there in that room with Maverick and that was all that mattered. I danced knowing that legally what we planned to do was wrong. But, where was the law when James beat me?

My marriage to James was simply a covenant on paper. My spiritual bond with Maverick transcended any sheet of paper issued by any judge. According to the law of attraction, the man who owned my heart would have the opportunity to caress it once more.

At midnight, Maverick and I left the masquerade party headed to his house. As we drove through the streets of Miami, traffic was slow, and the midnight air was calming. Fortunately, he didn't live far from the hotel. His home was a beachfront condo nestled in South Beach. We had danced so much that my soles were aching feverishly, and I was ready to get out of the red pumps I wore.

"Nice place," I said, as he opened the door, and his home welcomed me with open arms. A brown leather sectional centered the great room, which had a log cabin feel. I was thoroughly impressed with the unique décor.

"I try," he shrugged and offered me a seat on the sofa.

"Is this a full-size James Brown grandfather clock?" I asked.

He chuckled and said, "Yes. You never seen one like it?"

"Not exactly."

We talked about where he purchased the clock and about a few other sentimental pieces in his living room.

"My feet are killing me. Do you mind if I go put on something more comfortable?" I asked.

"Sure, babe. The bathroom is the first room on the left. I'll bring you a t-shirt and a pair of my boxers, if you feel you need them," he said with a sneaky smile.

I nodded and said, "That will be fine. Thanks."

Once in the shower, I lathered my towel with water and Dudu-Osun, a dark brown bar of African soap that had a rich earthy aroma. I recalled how much he loved to use that soap. I hated it when we were in college, but then it seemed perfect. Like him, it was unpretentious and pure. After drying off, I slipped into his oversized t-shirt and joined him in the living room. He was pouring a glass of water when I walked in.

"Would you like a glass of water?"

"Sure," I said, beginning to feel uneasy about being in his house and wearing his t-shirt. *I did say I wanted to spend the night with him,* I thought.

Memories of nights of hot passion, dreams of children, careers, marriage together, and hope for our future brought me comfort. His eyes met mine with reassurance and I knew I was in the right place with the right person at the right time. That man was my soul mate – el amor de mi vida.

It's not cheating if it is with your soul mate. That type of thing is just meant to be, I reasoned.

Matters of the heart trumped every guideline in the book. I reasoned there were certain raw emotions and passion that righted all wrongs, in all circumstances.

Those that made the breath we breathed more nourishing to the lungs and the food we ate more nutritious to the body. Some things were just meant to be.

He joined me on the couch and tossed back his cup of water in one gulp. "All of that dancing has me thirsty," he said.

"I know, right?" I took a few sips of my own drink. He took my glass from my hand and hugged me. I teasingly pushed him away. "Your shirt is soaking wet from all that dancing."

He ignored my statement and kissed me. "You never had a problem with me being sweaty before," he said, as he pulled his lips from mine.

"Yeah, but you're wet." I took him by the hand and said, "Come on, and let's get you out of these wet clothes."

I knew my way around his place enough to get him to the shower. We walked down his hallway and, when we were standing directly in front of his bed, I turned to face him and his tall frame towered over me. I drank in every contour of his chest as I unbuttoned his shirt, removed it, and then removed the t-shirt underneath. I kissed his chest before he tilted my head toward him and kissed me on the lips.

"I…I…I…" I wanted to say the words, but he pulled me close and wrapped his arms so tightly around my waist that I could barely breathe. The words caught in my throat.

He kissed me again, drowning out all thoughts and unspoken words. Heat traveled through my bones.

"Maverick!" I said, finally able to speak.

"Yes?" he said, lifting my shirt over my head and moving his kisses to my neck.

"I'm supposed to be getting you out of these wet clothes," I reminded him.

"Jesús dulce, usted no está usando ningunas bragas, Marisol! I'm going to get out of them," he said, as his wandering hands made note of the fact that I was not wearing any panties under the oversized tee.

"Te amo," he said. I loved it when he spoke in my native tongue to me. I felt like a woman granted an all-access pass to the world at large. I pushed him into the bathroom and turned on the shower. Within minutes, we were in bed where we stayed until sunrise.

Chapter 16

Rhonda

Sitting in my doctor's office, I had to do something to keep the voices in my head from driving me crazy. I was in a tailspin. Titus and Shayla had run off to California for Lord knows how long together to do Lord knows what. He had some nerve taking her and leaving me at home.

Ever since their plane left the ground, I was a wreck. California was our spot – the place he took me and could be his number one. When we went to Fa Ya Grillz, not only would I shop at some of the best stores in Beverly Hills, I was on his arm in front of his friends and acquaintances. The people that worked at that shop knew me as his woman. The thought of Shayla showing her high yellow-ass up and playing my position made me physically sick to the stomach.

I had coughed and threw up for three days in a row. For that reason, I was at my doctor's office for a checkup. I had to get something for my upset stomach or get my birth control pills changed, again. Ever since the doctor started me on a new brand last month, I had been cramping.

"Ugh! I hate that bitch!" I said clenching my teeth tightly together, as another wave of pain kicked me in the gut. I placed the magazine in my lap and sat still until the pain subsided.

Titus must had really been upset with me. He hadn't called or texted me since that stunt I pulled in his den. He would have been over it, if he wasn't running around with Shayla. I wondered what she did to get him to take her to California. I couldn't imagine her putting her foot down and making him take her.

With my stomach pain subsiding, I picked up the Essence of Color magazine from the rack. I skimmed through the pages until I found an interesting article about healthy relationships and lasting friendships. I thought about the irony of my current situation and the reading material in my hand. That writer was on a roll, talking about friends crossing the line. The part that got to me was:

> *We stick with people who support our social identity and withdraw from those who don't. We may even switch friends when the original ones don't support our current view of ourselves. Most of us would prefer to think that we love our friends because of who they are, not because of the ways in which they support who we are. It sounds vaguely narcissistic, and yet the studies bear it out.*

I looked up from the article and looked around the room. Was it possible that my friendship with Shayla was fading because she was not supporting me? Reading further down, the article began to talk about relationships.

> *A friend that is in a bad romantic relationship may be incapable of being a good friend. A lot of young women play down the hurtful things they do to their friends. While a person is dealing with unhealthy relationships, they are toxic to people who care about them the most. I want all of my readers to ask themselves, have your actions hurt people you love? What can you do to repair your relationships?"*

A moment of truth tugged at my subconscious. There I was upset that my best friend was on a trip with her husband. Sure, I loved her husband and slept with him every opportunity I got. But, I was convinced I was not the problem. They just were not meant for each other.

I sat there as if the article had jumped up and slapped me with the force of a moral hurricane. I wasn't trying to hear what the writer wrote in that article. I threw the magazine on the table with the rest of the know-it-all publications. I loved my friends the best way I knew how, all of three of them – Shayla, Gladys and Titus. It was just a different kind of love. I pulled out my mirror case from my cosmetic bag and looked at the woman staring back.

"I can't help that I love Titus in a special kind of way. It's not like I planned to be sprung over him like this. I don't know how to reverse it without losing a part of who I am," I said, looking hopelessly into the mirror.

A white woman sitting beside me looked at me like I was crazy. She held her child close to her as if she thought he would catch whatever mental disorder she thought I had. I rolled my eyes and put the mirror back in my cosmetic bag. I took out my cell phone to check my messages. There were none.

The nurse came out and said, "Ms. Jackson, you are up next. Dr. Swanman will see you in less than five minutes."

Eager to get my mind off my own dilemma, I made a quick call to Gladys. I wanted to see how her trip to Miami went. I was happy to hear her bubbly voice when she answered on the first ring.

"Hello! It is a great day at Naytek Corporation, Gladys speaking. How may I assist you?"

"Dang, girl. Work it then," I said, laughing as I spoke. I tried to sound full of energy and optimistic and not like the home-wrecking friend I was beginning to feel like. "I know you turned some heads down there with that two-piece we picked up at the mall last week. How was your trip?"

"I had fun. I may not have turned many heads, but I did turn one particular head."

"Aw snap, now you've got me curious. Who?"

"I will tell you when we get together with Shayla."

"She's in California with Titus and there is no telling when she will be back. I can't wait that long!"

"Well, take one guess. It's the last person you would ever expect." I didn't say anything for a few seconds, so she said, "He is from my college days at Albany."

No way, I thought. If she ran into the man I thought she was talking about, she was in trouble – good trouble. "No way, you saw Maverick Douglas?"

"Hell yes! And he was finer than three Morris Chestnuts in Speedos!" she said, with more life than I heard from her in years.

When she attended Albany State, Maverick Douglas was everything to Gladys. She was so in love with him that when she did come home on break, he was all she talked about. He brought out the best in her. When they broke up, she was so low on herself that she ended up settling for her trifling, cheating husband, James. She gave James all the chances she should have given Maverick. Her running into him was major.

"Oh my God! Tell me what happened. Did he say anything to you?" I asked.

"Yes, and he had me at hello. His voice, touch, and smell had me in a stronghold."

"Did you just say his touch had you in a stronghold, or was I hearing things? You know what, don't even answer that."

Gladys laughed. "It was good seeing him again. How did Shayla's big surprise shebang she planned for Titus turn out? I haven't talked to her since I got home."

"He didn't come home Friday night, so she was upset. The usual," I said, uninterested in going over the details of the past weekend again.

"I know she is hurt about that. She was excited about spending that time with her husband," Gladys said, and I could have sworn she put emphasis on 'her.'

When I didn't say anything, she continued, "She called me Friday morning all happy, bubbly and everything. He just never seems to do right. We gotta keep praying that she find the happiness and peace she deserves."

"Yeah, always. Well, they are in California now."

"Hopefully Titus is making it up to her in Cali. She deserves it." Gladys sure was laying the Shayla love on thick and it brought back my stomach pains.

"Well, I'm going to let you get back to your work," I said cutting her off.

"Okay, chica. I'll talk to you later," she said.

I hung up the phone feeling a little bit better. At least, I was a good friend to Gladys. The Essence of Color article I read had gotten it wrong.

I glanced at my watch and wondered what was taking the nurse so long to call me to the back.

Chapter 17

Shayla

The morning we got back from California, I woke up pleasantly surprised that my sleep had been so restful. Refreshed, I was ready to face that day head on. I went into the bathroom to wash my face.

"Today, I'm going to pamper myself some more," I said. After quality time with Titus, I felt all we needed was more time to grow our bond. I was sure that would remove him from the clutches of my so-called friend.

Within an hour, I dressed and headed to the beauty shop to get that cute little crinkly style he loved. After leaving the salon, I went to the nail shop for a quick pedicure, manicure, and facial. When I arrived back home, Titus was sitting in the den watching TV. I couldn't even describe the surprise of him being at home waiting on me, for a change.

"Hey, baby!" he said, as he stood up and walked to the door to greet me. He took the bag from my hand and placed it on the floor. He moaned and kissed my lips between words. "Damn, you look good. I almost didn't know what to do with myself while you were gone."

I had to admit that it felt good, at last. That was the man I fell in love with. That man made me feel that it was me, and only me, that made his heartbeat. In the back of my mind, I feared that his change was temporary. If so, I enjoyed it while it lasted.

"Flattery will get you everywhere," I said.

"I know." He squeezed my butt and said, "Hopefully, it will get me here."

I wiggled away from his grip and shook my index finger from side to side. "Not yet. You are going to spoil my surprise. Give me thirty minutes to freshen up, and I'll be right back."

"Aight, but don't make me wait too long. I'll pour up some of that wine we got from the refinery in Cali while I wait on your sexy ass to get back downstairs."

"Cool," I said, before dashing upstairs. Twenty minutes later, I sauntered into the room wearing a red lace bra, red G-string panties, and a pair of fire engine red six-inch heels. My lipstick was a red, as well. I could see his chest rise and fall with measured breaths as I walked toward him. It was nice to know that I made his breathing change.

Using the remote control, he turned off the TV and pressed the button to turn on the CD player. Sexual Healing by Al Green played through the speakers, which was the perfect song for the occasion. He was anxious, so he stood up and met me half way. He took me into his arms and placed butterfly kisses all over my face.

For a brief moment, I saw Rhonda receiving the same affection. I had to get out of that room, or else there was no way I would forgive or forget the despicable things he did with her in our den. An uncontrollable pain built in the pit of my stomach. It threatened to reveal itself through my tear ducts. Slowly, I backed away from him.

"Shayla, what's wrong?" he asked.

"Let's go upstairs."

***

Later that night, I sat at Mama Rosas waiting for Rhonda and Gladys. I was the first to arrive at the restaurant. Fifteen minutes later, I would sit face-to-face with the woman who called herself my friend while, at the same time, secretly enjoyed the flavor of my husband's body. I prepared myself for the phoniness of Rhonda's smile. She hadn't called or came by our house since that day.

It was Gladys' idea to have a girl's night out. We hadn't had one in a month, so it was time. She chose Mama Rosas as a central location where we all could meet and enjoy some of the best soul food. The family business was started with nothing but a dream and good food, and it attracted customers from all over the United States. I was sure I wouldn't bang Rhonda's head into a wall there. I respected Mama Rosa more than that.

Gladys said since she got back from Miami, things had taken a turn. Apparently, James was tripping. The

Florida sun worked wonders for my sister because, since she got back, he was being nice. She texted me the other day and said that he planned a family vacation, and the whole nine. She wanted us to get together, so we could discuss her situation. Since her husband had his act together, I wondered what the problem was.

Rhonda had no idea that I knew about her and Titus. But, what she would know by the end of the night was that we were in a new place in our marriage.

Gladys didn't know anything about her dirty deeds. If she caught wind of what Rhonda was doing, she would have told me in a heartbeat. She was a loyal friend.

Once I perfected a 'happy face' look, I checked my phone and saw Titus texted me three times already – one time to tell me that he missed me, a second time to tell me to hurry up and get back home, and a third time was just to say 'I love you.'

How sweet of him! I thought. Knowing I was about to sit face-to-face with Rhonda had caused his love to grow. If that wasn't guilt, I surely didn't know what was. I didn't respond to his messages.

"Hey, Sister-from-Another-Mother!" Gladys said, jarring me from my thoughts. Her face was lit up like a Christmas tree, and she basked in her new glow, smiling from cheek to cheek. Her silky hair flowed down her back. She wore a colorful sundress with matching sandals. She looked like a brand new woman.

"Hey, you! Your man must really be putting it on you!" I said, straight to the point. There were only a few things that could make a woman glow like that.

She slid into the seat beside me and gave me a one-arm hug. "Si, chica. Si! Is it that obvious? I have un nuevo amor? He is putting it down. I'm putting it down. We both are putting it doooooowwwwn." Gladys, giggled, at her own use of slang. She gave me a high five.

For the first time in years, I saw contentment in her like a well protected fort. It was the kind of happiness that was impermeable; nothing went in or out without permission.

I was happy she sat beside me. I sure as hell didn't want Rhonda sitting there. She would be forced to face me, which was exactly where I wanted to keep her from then on – in front of me. Not beside me and definitely not behind me with the big knife she carried around, ready to stab a sister in the back.

"I know my Spanish is a little rusty, but did you say nuevo amor?"

Gladys rolled her eyes and turned her head to the side.

"OMG! You look happier than I've seen you in years. Girl, now it all makes sense. You met someone in Florida."

"I *am* happy. Ronnie didn't tell you who I ran into in Miami?"

She was too busy screwing my husband to tell me anything, I thought. But, I said, "No, she didn't."

"Well, at least we know that girl can keep a secret," Gladys said.

Gladys had no idea how true her statement was. Rhonda knew how to keep a secret.

For the next ten minutes, she filled me in on the details of her time in Miami. She had no regrets, but felt like she let James and her kids down.

"I didn't know you had all of that on your plate. It will take time, but you will get through this. Trust me."

Just about the time she finished talking, Rhonda strolled into the restaurant wearing a Louis Vuitton cat suit, sunglasses, and a matching Louis Vuitton purse. It was the same outfit I purchased when I was planning the special evening for Titus. When we were in the store shopping, she told me that she didn't like the outfit and that 'it would make me look pudgy.' I could not believe she had the nerve to step off into Mama Rosas wearing that same damn outfit! I had wondered who financed the pricey things she owned. That day, the answer was loud and clear.

Rhonda beamed with artificial joy when she looked at me, as if she was actually glad to see me. "Hello, Sisters from Another Mama!" she said.

"Hi, girl," Gladys stood up and gave her a quick hug. I watched the exchange and my stomach turned. Rhonda could be so phony. Knowing her, she probably slept with James, too.

Rhonda slid into the booth in front of me, and said, "Hey, Shayla. What – are you not speaking?"

I looked her dead in the eye without saying a word. Finally, I said, "Hey."

"Okay... So, how did you and Titus enjoy your trip to California?"

"It was lovely, every minute of it. We went to a few landmarks in Hollywood. I shopped on Rodeo Drive and rode the trolley to tour some of the most influential stars homes. Then, hubby surprised me with tickets to P. Diddy's All White Affair. It was one *beautiful experience* after another, if you know what I mean."

I scattered, smothered, and covered her face with details of our trip. I gave Gladys a high five for added effect.

"He said he never had so much fun in Cali, and neither had I."

"Oh, that's nice," Rhonda said and conveniently changed the subject. "Well, we're here to help our girl, so I'm assuming you told Shayla everything?" she said to Gladys.

A blind person could see the friendly tension between us. Gladys looked back and forth between Rhonda and me.

"Yes, I just told her about it before you came in," she said.

"So, what are you going to do?" Rhonda asked. "He is such a *dog!*"

Sitting there with a woman who was in my den sucking my husband's dick a week ago had my skin boiling. I couldn't help but ask, "You know a dog when you see one, don't you Rhonda?"

"Huh?" they both replied at the same time.

"Never mind." I waved my hand dismissing the statement.

Gladys spoke to Rhonda, but kept her gaze fixed on me questioning me with her eyes. "I-I don't know,

Rhonda. My heart says leave him and don't look back, but my conscience tells me that I will regret it."

"Well, here are some things for you to think about. One, you've only spent one weekend with Maverick. While you knew him in college, fast forward to eight years later, and you don't know him from a can of paint. Sure, you had a magical weekend, and all of that is nice, but that doesn't mean he is man enough to take care of you and your kids. That also does not mean he is sane. He could be a crazy stalker that will end up worse than James in the long run." I had to give Gladys some news that Rhonda's airheaded ass would be too naïve to tell her. Of course, she was on Cloud Nine after a weekend with Maverick, but eight years can really change a brother.

"Shay has a point," Rhonda agreed. She avoided eye contact and focused solely on Gladys.

"I know he could have changed, but Shayla, you didn't experience what I did. You didn't see the genuineness flowing from his soul to mine. When he kissed me, when he said my name, and when he whispered Spanish love messages into my ear until I went to sleep, it was all real. He is the same man I was in love with then, if not better. The feelings are still there and are super strong, just as strong as they were back at Albany. I'm mature enough to know the difference but, for the sake of my children, I will take it slow. Hell, if it were just me and no children, I would be calling you guys from Florida right now."

I turned to her and said, "Well, if the feelings have been there for eight years, they will be there next year and the following year. Those feelings are not going anywhere anytime soon, especially after what you shared last weekend. Therefore, you can hold out a little while longer before you divorce James, uproot the children, and move to Miami because of one great encounter. Come on, Gladys, you are a smart girl. Put your thinking cap on. "

With that cheesy grin that was starting to irritate me, Rhonda opened her mouth to speak. "Yeah, you ain't got to be trying to run down there and marry his ass. Why not just creep with him? You know, get your groove on in Miami once a month or something like that. Maverick could even come and meet you up here sometimes. There are ways to handle your business on the down low, ya know?" she raised her eyebrows as if she was giving a hint.

That was it! I was about to snatch her wig off. The nerve of her to give advice on how to creep.

"I guess I could get my creep on," Gladys said ambivalently.

"You could do that, or you could divorce James and take it slow with Maverick. That is all I'm saying. Get to know him again. Date him. Let your kids get to know him, and you get to know how he is with your kids. Then you can make your next move. Don't end up being on the sidelines because you didn't do things the right way. You're not some low-class jumpoff that has to take that route, Gladys." I looked at Rhonda as I said the last line, because it was for her to comprehend.

Rhonda said, "When you find something good like what you have with Maverick, you have to take the bull by the horns and just go for what you want – no matter what or *who* the obstacle is."

That sideline ho was talking about me. I was done. I would never look at her like a sister of mine. She crossed every imaginary line in the sand drawn. She was officially on the enemy line.

"Every obstacle is not meant to cross," I said, and Rhonda and I went tit for tat for the next hour or so, coaching Gladys on her situation.

I took a good look at my two friends' situations. Gladys was creeping on her husband who was constantly creeping on her. My husband was creeping around with Rhonda who was my best friend. Was I the only one in my circle without a secret?

Chapter 18

Shayla

"It's discouraging to think how many people are shocked by honesty and how few are shocked by deceit." As I mapped out today's events, I found the amazing quote I read last week by Noel Coward rather fitting.

At the first each month, Titus and his crew collected money owed to them and flipped cash. It was the day a lot of their customers got paid, so in essence it was their payday, as well. I loved that day. I didn't have to worry about him, or any of his goons, snooping around in my business.

I got out of bed around seven in the morning, brushed my teeth, and poured a tall glass of water. I had a few things to check on. If my suspicion was correct, that day was as good as any to set it off. I dressed in a peach form-fitting tank top, Bermuda Gucci pants with the matching Gucci black shades, Gucci purse, and Gucci shoes, to boot. Back in my bedroom, I surveyed myself in the mirror. I was a natural born showstopper.

"Thank God, I don't look like what I've been through," I said to no one in particular. With my swagger at one hundred and twenty percent, I collected my purse, keys and shades from my dresser and hit the road. My naturally wavy hair bounced in the wind as I crossed the Alabama-Georgia line on I-85 headed to Lee County. The crisscross twists that my stylist designed in the front if my hair were absolutely gorgeous.

I had not heard from Rhonda in three weeks and Titus hadn't been home in two days. For the first time since I caught him red handed with her, he didn't come home or call for an entire weekend. And when I called him – just like the bad ole' days – my calls went straight to voicemail.

I called Street to find out what was going on, but he said Titus had some business to handle. If that was true, why couldn't he just pick up the phone and tell me that? I could tell Street was caught off guard when I called because he had a hard time putting that story together. I had a pretty good notion that Rhonda's house would be where he was. Her upscale townhouse division on the north side of Auburn was my destination. Every time I asked her how she could afford to live in that townhouse, she would say, "I have my ways."

I bet she had one way. Mr. Wilson. I sent up a silent prayer as I pulled into her apartment complex. I prayed to God above that I would not find his car in the parking lot.

"Lord, please don't let my husband's car be here," I said, hoping for a tiny bit of leniency from the powers up above. That was the first time in years I had gone out checking behind Titus. I prayed that neither of my husband's cars would be in my best friend's parking lot. But, sure enough, his car was not only on the lot, it was parked directly in front of Rhonda's door, as if it was his own personal parking space. If he was comfortable enough to do that, at least half of the town, if not everyone in town, knew about it.

I sat in the car in a daze. My attention was fixed on Rhonda's front door. I could see her pinned against the living room wall as he kissed her. I could see her pleasing him in the same way I saw on our home security tape. We had a security system installed when we moved in and the tapes verified what my eyes didn't see. Knowing that Titus was so sloppy made me wonder how I miss all the signs in the first place. I knew Rhonda was scandalous when she went under the bleachers with Carlton. It wasn't like I was in love with him. However, it was messed up that she had sex with him and didn't have the decency to tell me about their little escapade. It took a random female to tell me about the bleacher ordeal. At that time, I didn't want to believe it, so said what's done in the dark always comes to light.

"This should be an interesting confrontation," I said as I sat in the car. Once my heart rhythm returned to normal and my breathing went from erratic to calm, I shut off the car engine and gave myself a once over in the mirror. Finding the confidence to complete my mission, I gave myself a quick pep talk.

"Go on and handle your business, Shay. What they are doing is foul," I told myself.

I opened the car door, got out, and walked to Rhonda's front door. I knocked. The blinds quickly rose and fell, but no one answered. After a minute or two of beating on the door, there still wasn't an answer. My blood pressure shot up and I saw red.

I knocked harder and screamed, "Ronnie, I know you're in there, so open the damn door! Tell my husband to get out here, now."

I heard things bumping around inside of the apartment. Attempting to steady my voice, I bellowed, "Your cars are out here, Titus and Rhonda. I saw you peeping out the blinds, so open up this door!"

I had a twisted hope that Titus had a good explanation for being there. I wanted him to tell me something believable regarding why I found him at Rhonda's apartment. The hard truth was too painful.

I heard my husband's groggy morning voice ask, "What's that noise, baby?"

To say that I was enraged hearing him ask her that question would be an understatement. Suddenly, the rage blew up inside of me and, before I knew anything, I rammed the door with my full body. I was about to lose my natural born mind.

"Open up this door, Rhonda! Titus!" I demanded, banging as quickly as my little hands would move. I heard Rhonda tell Titus, "It's her."

"Who?"

"Shayla."

"Shit!" he said before opening the door like he was the man of the house. Calm and collected, as if he was *supposed* to be there at nine in the morning, he stroked loose strands of my hair back into place and said, "Heeeeeyyy, babe! What are you doing over here?"

I quickly yanked away from him. "What am I doing here? Motherfucker, what are you doing here?"

I turned my attention to Rhonda. "You are messing with the wrong one. You have worse things coming to you in life than eating second off my plate. I was a true friend to you, for years! I loved you like you were my blood, and gave you all I had. And this – sleeping with my husband – is how you repay me?"

"Chile, what's love got to do with it?" Rhonda said, waving her hand in the air like she didn't care.

Titus stepped in front of me, but I got away from him and was all in Rhonda's face. I wanted her to say one more word, and it was going to be a massacre in that house.

She stood there in a pink negligee and threw her hands in the air. She walked off and said, "Titus you need to handle this."

"Oh, no you didn't! Don't you tell my husband what to do and then walk away from me. I'm not done with you yet." I rushed to catch her, but Titus grabbed my arm.

He stroked my hair again, as if he possessed the power to calm me down. I yanked my arm nearly out of the socket to get it away from his hold.

"Shayla, calm down. You're out of line," he said.

"Negro, please! You have not been home all weekend and I find you at Rhonda's house? She's wearing practically *no* clothing when you open her front door. And you think that is in line? Bright and early Monday morning, you're over here and got the nerve to ask me what *I'm* doing here? What are *you* doing here? Don't even answer that. I know the answer!"

As soon as Titus wasn't standing between us, I planned to school Rhonda on some things. He was fully dressed in his black Ecko T-shirt and jeans, black Timberlands and Atlanta Falcon cap. But, Rhonda's pink silk negligee barely covered her legs. While he held me back, she had gone to her bedroom and came back up the hall wearing sweat pants and a t-shirt. She must have put on some nerves in her bedroom, too, because she jumped in our conversation.

"Shayla, you are over reacting, as usual, sweetie. Calm down, and let the man speak, and maybe you'll know something. Otherwise, you are going to have to keep it moving with the drama, and get up out of here."

She stood in my face like everything was honky dory, as if she was not just standing in he same spot with a pink negligee, shear robe, NO PANTIES, and hot pink stilettos. And, I hated when people called me "sweetie" in the middle of a disagreement.

Titus and Rhonda were ready for the Oscars. They both acted as if I was the fool. I stepped out of the sandals I wore. A millisecond away from going to work on her scurvy ass, I grabbed a patch of her hair and said, "You really don't know me like you think you do!"

She squirmed trying to get out of my grasp. "There is nothing going on with us. Let me go. It's me, Shayla, your girl," she lied through her man-sucking teeth.

Titus maneuvered my fingers out of her hair and said, "Calm down, Shayla. Now!"

"Fuck you, Titus," I screamed, outdone with the whole situation.

"Shayla, babe, don't talk like that. That's not you. You need to get back in place. Quick." He took my hand firmly, coaxing me back to the reality that I didn't want the situation to get too far out of control where the police were called, and we were all arrested.

"Now, if you will take a few minutes to listen, I will tell you why I am here. Rhonda has been helping me plan a surprise birthday party for you. This morning, I was on my way home and swung by here to give her this money for the entertainment. I'm getting Joe to come out to sing to you."

He held up an envelope with money in it and looked at me like I was supposed to get excited about the news. Instead, my temples throbbed.

When I didn't show any emotion, he continued, "I can't have nothing but the best for my baby, and Rhonda is helping me with the plans. Now you've gone and spoiled your surprise party."

He licked his lips and intertwined his fingers in mine. He was nonchalant like he didn't have a care in the world. That little act of his beat all I'd ever seen. A surprise birthday party, really?

I played along with it, because I didn't go over to Rhonda's house to lose my husband. Much to the contrary, I went over there to take him home.

"You came by to give her money for entertainment, huh? Are you sure you didn't give her money for *her* entertaining *you.* I mean, she was dressed in her hooker clothes." I looked at Rhonda and added, "Just like hookers do."

"Now you wait a damn minute, Shay. Don't come in here throwing accusations around in my house. I ain't sleeping with your husband or even trying to get with him like that. He came over here to give me the money for your party, so there is no reason for you to take whatever insecurities you have out on me. He is *your* husband and is doing something for *you*, so handle your business with him at your house."

My best friend was a pro. Her speech was pretty darned convincing. If I didn't know any better, I would have believed every word coming out of her mouth.

Despite the evidence I already had, I was open to accept one more of his explanations. I desperately wanted things to go back to the way they were before the money went to everybody's heads. I told Titus, "It sounds a little shady, considering that you usually handle your own business. Tell me what is going on, for real. Make me feel better about this."

I wanted to reach the man that knew the true meaning of love. I wanted my friend that knew the meaning of friendship to show up in that room. I needed Titus to say something that would give me the strength to destroy the tape and wipe the slate clean.

All of that hoping and wishing he would form the perfect words to say was diminished when Rhonda let out an exasperated sigh.

"Don't beat around the bush, Shayla. For once in your life, just come on with it."

I wondered if she ready to lay all of the cards on the table. The look on her face told me she was tired of the cat and mouse games, as well.

"You heard my *wife*," Titus said in an attempt to nip the exchange in the bud. "My baby wanted to know what's going on, so she gets to know what's going on. Whatever wifey wants, wifey gets. It's just too bad I had to spoil the surprise party, but it's all good."

He glared at Rhonda daring her to say another word. I knew that look. Actions definitely spoke louder than words.

He took me by the hand and said, "I have been missing you and then you come in here acting up. I see we have a lot to talk about when we get home."

Fed up to my neck, I slid back into my sandals. I told Titus, "Yes, we do have a lot to talk about. I think you should meet me at home."

The two people that were supposed to have my back in the world were still performing surgery on my spine with their double-headed dagger. As far as I was concerned, Titus and Rhonda crossed the line from friends to enemies over a month ago. But, I still loved my enemies. I swallowed the lump in my throat and walked out of her apartment with Titus close behind.

He was my husband, and as sad as the situation was, I still loved him. The fact that I successfully retrieved him from Rhonda's claws was enough for that moment.

Chapter 19

Gladys

I didn't see Brenda the entire weekend I was in Florida. I dialed her cell phone, and for the first time, she picked up on the first ring.

"Hi, Brenda! It's Gladys." I said.

"Hi Gladys."

"I must tell you that your setup in MIA was off the hook! The party was fabulous, and it's a shame I didn't run into you the whole weekend. I tried calling you while I was there, so we could meet up, but you must have been busy."

"What are you talking about? I haven't been to Miami in years."

I dropped the pencil I held and stared intently at the phone as if it had some explaining to do. I remembered running into several of my African American studies classmates while in Florida, so I knew Brenda must have been pulling my leg. There was no way she was senile enough to forget her own party.

"But, you just threw a party down there two weeks ago for our classmates. The masquerade party at the Fontainebleau Resort?"

"No, Gladys. As much as I'm dying to travel, I haven't been outside of New York City in three years. They have me down here working like a Hebrew slave getting things in order for a new study program. It has been all work and no play for Brenda J."

Rubbing my temples to relieve the stress growing there, I asked once more to be sure, "So, you didn't send me an invite to Miami?"

"Um, that would be a negative."

My voice began to tremble as the weirdness of the situation sank in. "Okay, well, thanks for clearing that up. I guess I have myself a little mystery to figure out. I have an idea of which direction to aim my investigation, though."

"Good luck with that. In the mean time, help me spread the word by letting all of your friends know that the African American Leaders of the World study program will be going global soon. I will send you an email with further details to share with the other execs at your company. This is an exciting progressive movement that I know your company will want to cosign on as it will undoubtedly bring more exposure to Naytek."

"As soon as I get the info in my hands, it's a done deal, girl. I will get the information to the CEO. She is very progressive and always looking to help other black businesswomen. I will get back with you on the details when I've talked to her." With that said, we said our goodbyes.

The phone slid back onto the console on its own. I was confused with the information she laid on me. I called Shayla who answered on the second ring.

"Hello," she answered, sounding sad. I could hear water running and dishes moving around.

I took a deep breath and said, "Shayla, are you near a chair?"

"Oh, no. Should I be?"

"Please sit down, so you can help me sort some things out."

"Okay, I'm sitting down. What's up?"

"First of all, when I called Brenda Jackson to thank her for the Miami getaway hookup, she said she didn't send the invitation."

I stood up and walked over to look out of my large office window. Cars thirty feet below were bustling through the digested Atlanta downtown traffic. Everyone knew exactly where they were going. Yet, I was stuck in place in my office wondering what my next move would be.

"What....? Well, who sent it?" Shayla asked.

"I have no idea."

"That is strange."

"Very strange. She was clueless about the whole Florida thing. She said she had not been out of New York City in three years, so there was no way she could have invited me to a party in Miami."

Shayla said, "Oh." It was apparent she was just as confused as I was about the whole ordeal. "So, I wonder who concocted the whole Brenda-Jackson-is-throwing-a-party-in-Florida deal."

"I have a pretty good idea of the direction to start in, but I do *not* know why he would try to get me down there under false pretenses."

"Maverick?"

"Exactamundo!"

"You think he set the entire weekend up?"

I walked back to my chair and buried my head into my free hand. "At first, I was surprised at the *coincidence* that we ended up in the same place at the same time with the same amount of passion burning for each other, but knowing that Brenda didn't do it goes against coincidence."

"How would you feel if you knew he was the one that arranged it all, using Brenda's name as an alias, to get you there?"

"I don't know how to feel about that. I'll know how I feel after I call him to get this cleared up." I was about to say my goodbyes, but Shayla cut me off.

"Do you want to know what I think you should do?"

"Sure, what would my sister do?"

"First of all, I think it was a *very* sweet gesture of Maverick's and knowing that he set the entire thing up makes for a nice a romantic tale. Setting him up to sweep you off your feet and steal you away from your everyday grind to give you a magical weekend... A weekend that you said yourself you will never forget. I think you should be happy that he cared enough to do all of that for you is what I'm trying to say."

"And Shayla, trust me I *am* happy. But, this changes the dynamics of everything. Sure, it's a sweet gesture, but I'm the type that likes to know what's up without too many surprises, you know? If he'll lie about something as special as our reason for reuniting, what else has he lied about?"

That thought touched a chord. My mind was full of questions, and my heart was tugging in different directions. Should I be happy? Should I be disappointed? Was it possible to be both at the same time? I felt a sense of déjà vu upon me – was I finding another reason to get angry at Maverick just when things were going well, just like back in college? Could I be setting myself up for a fall again, possibly risking losing the best thing that ever happened to me, besides my children?

"Well, let me know as soon as you talk to Maverick. On a lighter note, make sure you are at my *surprise* party Saturday, bright and early, and dressed to impress. I need you there, because I don't know what Rhonda and Titus are up to with planning this thing."

"I will be there, and don't I always dress to impress?" We laughed at the inside joke. Shayla was always teasing me about the way I dressed. Then, she became silent and I realized I was the only one laughing.

"Gladys?" she asked, sounding as if something was bothering her suddenly.

"Yeah, honey?"

Instead of answering, she quickly brushed it off, and said, "That's okay."

"Are you sure you don't have something on your mind, Shayla?"

"I'm sure. I'll talk to you later," she said before adding, "love you."

"I love you, too." And with that said, we hung up. I had an important call to make to Mr. Douglas.

Chapter 20

Shayla

Ding, dong! I woke to the sound of the doorbell. I walked down the stairwell and peeped through the living room curtains. There was a man holding cleaning supplies at the door and a *Rent a Pool Guy* truck in the driveway.

"May I help you?" I said through the window.

"Your husband hired me to service your pool today."

"Damn," I whispered under my breath and disabled the alarm. I was too sleepy to deal with pool maintenance that morning. Then, I remembered Titus had wanted to have the pool area serviced before my party. I opened the door and a Hispanic young man that sounded too chipper to be out doing his job so early in the morning walked into the foyer. His Spanish roots were evident as he spoke. His shiny black hair was pulled back in a ponytail.

"Oh, that's right. We were expecting you," I lied, because I had completely forgotten. Titus told me about the appointment after I pulled him out of Rhonda's apartment.

Titus' baby cousin, Tanya, referred Antonio because he was one of her classmates at the local community college. He did maintenance as a side business along with working part time at a local department store. Titus liked the young man's hustle, so he hired him to clean our pool area up for the party. Once he stepped into the foyer, I checked him out from head to toe. He was young, built nice, and easy on the eyes.

"I hope you are having a good morning, Mrs. Wilson?"

"I'm fine, and you?"

"I won't complain. Which way to your pool?" he asked. He really was a cutie.

"Oh, where are my manners? Good morning and it's right this way." I walked ahead of him in the direction of the patio side door. "The pool is out this door. When you want to come back in, ring the buzzer, and I will come down and let you in.

"Yes ma'am," he said, and from the grin on his face, he had watched my hips move from side to side as I walked.

After getting him squared away, I stood beside the patio window and watched him work. After all, I had to make sure he did things right since it was his first day on the job. A tiny voice told me to stop watching him, but I ignored that voice and watched his tanned obliques and sexy legs work for the next few hours. I popped a bowl of popcorn, sat in my lounger, and watched him like a movie.

The sun beamed down so hard that he took off his t-shirt and exposed his firm chest. When he took his shirt off, I couldn't take it any longer. I got up to go take a cool shower and get dressed.

When I returned downstairs, I took him a glass of freshly squeezed lemonade so he would not get dehydrated. I didn't know where he was from, but I introduced him to southern hospitality.

"Antonio, you have been working nonstop since you got here. Take a break and have a glass of lemonade with me." The sunshine reflecting off his skin was a glimpse of heaven. Yes, that would be his nickname from now on *Sunshine.*

Fantasizing about him being *my* sunshine could only lead to trouble, so I pushed the thought out of my mind.

"On the second hand, I know you have a lot of work to do, so I'll just leave the lemonade on the patio table for you to drink whenever you're ready for a break."

His face lit up as if a cool drink was just what the doctor ordered. "Thanks, Mrs. Wilson. I'll take a quick break now."

"Okay, well, I'll be inside if you need anything." I went into the house ready to get out of reach of that hunk of a man. Three hours after he started the job, he rang the buzzer to come back inside.

"We didn't leave it in too much of a mess, did we?" I asked, knowing a bad thunderstorm had destroyed the pool cover two months ago.

Flexing the muscles in his chest, he said, "I had my work cut out for me, but I got the job done."

"And you did an excellent job, so when can I expect you back?" My face turned flush red with embarrassment as soon as I asked that question. He completed the job and lo' and behold I was trying to get him to come back.

He wrote some numbers down on his receipt book and then handed me a bill. "Even with the cover destroyed, it wasn't in that bad of shape. It looks like you take great care of the pool. Plus, with the bottom made of marble, it won't need that much care. I could come back next month just to check everything out."

Holding the bill up, I said, "That sounds good. Wait here just a second." I walked into the kitchen and got my checkbook. I wrote the check out for one hundred dollars more than the invoice and handed it to him.

"Unless you need the pool cleaned out sooner than my one month check? I have no problem coming back over here as many times as you need me to," he said.

"I'll just see you next month," I said.

"Okay, you have a beautiful day, Mrs. Wilson."

"You, as well," I said, ushering him to the door.

As soon as I closed the door behind him, I exhaled a deep sigh. Oh, God, I have too much confusion in my life to add a pool guy!"

I made a mental note to be in the first pew at church that Sunday. It had been months since I saw momma, so I knew she would be too ecstatic to see me at church. Searching my heart of hearts, I knew the Godly thing to do would be to bring my friends with me. They both were fighting their own demons. We all, in one way or another, were fighting demons and losing the battle.

Gladys filed for divorce. She said it was not so she could be with Maverick, but because her relationship with James was toxic. The fact that Maverick was back in the picture didn't hurt either. When James went one step too far, hitting her in front of their daughter, she took his death threats seriously and filed for divorce. The last thing she wanted was for James to show Nazaria that men should beat her, or worse, kill her. That was not the way she wanted her children to learn to love. I was proud of her for making that move. She never told me James was physical with her, but when he made that drastic mistake, she called me in tears and revealed the whole story. Thank God, she found the strength to take herself and her children out of that situation.

As far as Rhonda, I hadn't talked to her much over the past week. I guessed she didn't like that Titus spent more time at home. Gladys had not figured out that Rhonda and I were on bad terms, but she told me that Rhonda was going back and forth to the doctor with stomach pains. I refused to call her and check on her. I couldn't fake the funk about our friendship, no matter how hard I tried.

Chapter 21

Rhonda

Party Time

We were all in the kitchen preparing drinks. It was the only place in the house that wasn't swarmed with people. Shayla walked around in this cute little Baby Phat sleeveless dress number acting as if she didn't know me from a can of paint. I noticed she talked to Gladys, but to me – *nada.*

"Girl, what is your problem? You have been acting salty towards me all day," I said. It was the day of her birthday party, and she acted as if her shit didn't stink – throwing dip bowls in the sink and moving around me as if she had not heard me talking to her. I didn't care much at all for her attitude.

"I didn't have to set up your little party if you were going to treat me worse than the help!" I said.

Shayla met my eyes with an emotionless expression. Then, she continued to prepare the drinks for the waiting guests. I grabbed a wine cooler and drank half of it in one long gulp.

"Whatever..." I huffed under my breath. If she wanted it to be that way, it would stay that way.

Since Titus gave the phony story about throwing her a party, he had to follow through with it. We got that "surprise party" organized in one week's time. He managed to pool together his resources and connections to get the singer Joe to come out and do three songs to set the night off right.

I was on pins and needles waiting for Joe to get his sexy butt to the house. I went to several concerts for performers before, but I'd never had the opportunity to mix and mingle with a star of his caliber in an impersonal setting. That was going to be a treat! I hoped he would cheer Shayla's high-rolling butt up.

I'd noticed for the past month or so that she really was on point with keeping her look tight. There was not one time that I saw her dress average. Even though I wouldn't tell her, she had it going on. I knew how much Titus cared about her and I was sure that he took notice of her appearance.

Another thing bothering me was that she popped up at my house last week showing out. She obviously was on to something that she hasn't admitted. A real woman never spilled all of her beans, and Shayla was holding something in. Either way, she messed up my groove with Titus. I was about to give him one for the road when she blew up my spot.

Ever since she caught us like that, he hadn't been back to my apartment. While she stood at the sink chatting away with Gladys, I wished I could erase her from existence. She was the only thing standing between me and happiness.

I left out of the kitchen and went to find Titus. People were in the living room, dining room, and hallway, but the pool was where most of the action was. Alcohol was plentiful, and the smell of dank filled the air. It was a typical Titus party – People, beer, liquor, food, dank, and chips – nothing but a G-thang, baby.

Within a week's time, we managed to invite two hundred guests, and it seemed like everyone we had invited had brought along a friend or two. There were two spades games going on, and Street was on a winning streak, betting anyone that thought they knew how to play that if they sat down as his opponent they would leave the table minus a couple of Gs. I could tell Street did most of the invites, because there were women for days walking around barely dressed and tatted up like gangstettes.

Everyone was chilling until Shayla came out and pulled Titus to the side. Shayla didn't like it when he smoked in the house, so her corny butt was straight tripping on the other people smoking in the house. I was not far behind him when he walked into the kitchen with her.

"Titus, baby take these drinks out to the cooler," Shayla said. When he reached her to take the drinks from her hand, she whispered, "And you need to tell your friends no smoking in the house."

I grinned from ear to ear, knowing he would let her know that he was the man of their house. Instead of him telling her to stay in her place, he kissed her cheek and simply said, "Done deal."

I couldn't believe my ears. Whatever that bitch said was the gospel. He puckered up and kissed her ass every time she opened her mouth. As far as I was concerned, there was nothing wrong with the people smoking in the house. It was a party and people were there to have fun. I had to get out of there.

Watching them be all lovey dovey with each other was too much. I walked into the pantry to find some cups to put on the drink table. Anything to be out of view of him acting like he was in love with her. When I got back into the kitchen, they were snuggled up by the sink.

Newsflash – whenever a couple is overly affectionate around others, acting like they are so in love that all they can do is cuddle and kiss, there is usually more to the story. The act of cuddling, kissing, groping, and lusting after each other in public settings is for the public to get the impression that they are happy. I was hip to the game of putting on airs for the benefit of others, and I wasn't buyin' it. I knew better – End Newsflash.

I placed the cups on the counter and looked past them into the living room. I saw that no one was smoking inside anymore and that all of the festivities had made their way outdoors. If it were up to her, Titus' bomb-ass parties would be whack as hell. We'd probably all be sitting around playing Charades and Yahtzee and sipping on sodas and iced tea.

"How are my niece and nephew?" I asked Gladys.

"Into everything, as usual," she flippantly answered before putting her drink on the counter. "What's wrong with you today? You seem tense about something," she asked.

"I'm cool. Everything is cool. What's going on with you and Maverick?"

"Honey, you should be asking me what isn't going on with Maverick. *Er'thang* is going on with him."

We laughed out loud at her extraness.

"I called him and told him Brenda didn't send me the arrangements for the Miami weekend. He was like 'Oh, so you talked to her?' So I said, 'Yes, and what I need to know from you is did you send me the masquerade party invitation and free hotel nights?'"

"What did he say?" I asked, anxiously, beginning to like Maverick more and more by the minute. He was a romantic slickster, a very nice combination. He reminded me of someone I knew very well – me.

"Girl, he didn't deny a thing. He had perused my Linked-Online profile and reviewed my company profile. Then, one day he stopped through Auburn for gas and ran into my aunt. After he got all of the information he needed from mi tía Cindy, including where I worked and phone numbers, he went into planning mode. He said, 'I know how you used to love Brenda's parties, so I figured if I had any chance at getting you to Florida it would be through an invitation from her.'"

"And it worked too," I giggled and got a few warm feelings from their love connection. "But I can't believe your aunt Cindy gave up all your info like that. That is so much like her. She's never met a stranger."

"Yes! But you know the funny thing is that with the way things were with James before I reconnected with Maverick, I would have gone to meet him if he sent the invite himself. I told him that. He didn't have to trick me into meeting him. He had me at hola, girl."

"I know you would have gone, and you shouldn't feel bad about the feelings you have for him, either. Life's experiences have a way of forcing us to challenge each and every one of our principles. We can't help who we love," I said, as a somberness came over me that I never experienced before. I quickly recovered, but it was too late.

She looked all concerned and motherly and pursed her lips. "Is there anything you want to tell me, Rhonda?"

"Of course not, things couldn't be better."

About that time, Shayla walked into the room. "Y'all are talking about Maverick," she said.

Smiling ear to ear, Gladys answered, "Yeah, I told her about his trick and how much I love him for it."

Shayla looked at me pointedly, and said, "You know when a man loves a woman for years like Maverick has loved you, there is nothing, and *no one*, that will keep them apart."

"Ain't that the truth!" Gladys said, giving Shayla a high five.

I was about to respond with my two cents when a loud commotion coming from the living room interrupted me. People screamed out and cheered for Joe who came through the door singing Happy Birthday to Shayla. Titus took his place beside her as Joe sang his heart out. He looked at her in a way he never did look at me while whispering in her ear. When Joe sang Shayla's name, Titus mouthed it along with him, and she wiped away a tear from the corner of her eye. All the women in the room went crazy. Some held their hands to their hearts while some whispered to their friends that they wished it were them being serenaded. When he was finished singing, he handed Titus the mic and said, "I think you have something to say to your girl."

"Thank you, bruh. Yeah, I definitely do." Titus smiled, gazing into Shayla's moist eyes. He wrapped his arms around her waist while Joe and all of the party-goers looked on.

Looking around the room, I saw Gladys staring at me with her eyebrows furrowed. I wondered if my disgust was that obvious. She tipped her head at me questioningly, but I ignored her and watched my man embrace his mismatched wife.

"Shayla, I hope this party shows you how much you mean to me. I know Joe is your favorite singer and I would have nothing less than the best come sing Happy Birthday to my wife on her special day. You're my world, girl, and I want you to be happy. You're always number one, two, and three in my book, Shay. I love you, forever."

While the crowd clapped and cheered and I heard Joe begin to sing again, I slipped out of the room and ran to the nearest toilet to unload the bile that rushed into my throat.

Chapter 22

Titus

Because I did most of the planning for the party, Shayla didn't know half the guests. I invited some of her folks, but her mother told me to stop calling her sanctified ass family. She said they would rot in hell before they ate at the table with drug dealers. Not spending time with their blood was on them because my baby was going to have the best with or without their Bible toting butts in attendance. Rhonda was supposed to contact all of Shayla's friends she was connected to, but she did a piss poor job of getting them out to the party. With the way she'd been acting, she probably didn't even reach out to any of them. No one in their right mind would miss a party thrown by Titus Wilson, so I knew she couldn't have put any effort into getting the word out.

Shayla did know that sanging ass nigga, Joe. I wasn't going to be the one to start screaming and hollering because he was up in my house singing. However, I was proud that, once again, I'd shown these niggas how I much I was on another level. I did it big up in that piece. Even though I paid him for three songs, he was all up in my woman's face on his fourth song singing to the top of his lungs. I slipped my arm around her waist and pulled her close. I pulled her so close that the smell of my cologne reminded her who she belonged to. She looked away from Joe and smiled at me. I knew she was satisfied and that was all I wanted. I owed her that on her birthday. After the singing was done, Joe mingled for a little bit before he signed a few autographs and bounced.

The Street Justice crew was all the way live with diamonds glistening in their ears, swinging platinum chains, and fresh threads from the head to the feet. We were platinum boys from the hood. That was how we did it.

I looked at my watch, and it was nine o'clock, so I hollered, "Time for the all-white bikini jam! I want all of you ladies out of those clothes and in the pool in fifteen. Fellows, do what you do in your all white swimming trunks."

It was all about the white. No dirty bitches or niggas were allowed to hang around in my spot.

When Shayla sashayed her fine butt to the pool with her all-white, string bikini it was game over for any female that thought about putting on a swimsuit that night. Baby was banging! I gave her a twirl, and said, "Look at all that booty! Is all of this for me?"

"If you want it," she said teasingly and wiggled from my embrace.

"You know I want it," I said pulling her back to my side. I reveled in the beauty she exuded, and all of her glory. I didn't know if she would make it into the pool wearing that bikini like that. I was two seconds away from pulling a Marty-Mar and telling everyone, "You ain't got to go home, but you got to get the hell up outta here!"

"Do I?" she asked with a smile that turned to disgust when Sheniqua flaunted in front of me wearing a microscopic bikini top. It wasn't even a real bikini, just four pieces of string connected to two little patches covering her nipples.

"Great party, big Tee," she said without addressing my wife. She rubbed my chest when she spoke. No doubt, she was looking to score a baller, but it would not be me. I wasn't feeling the way she disrespected Shayla, in our house. I popped my knuckles and raised an eyebrow at her. She got the picture and walked away.

Shayla gave me that look and I knew she was not feeling the women who walked around acting like they had some type of relations with me.

Pulling her close, I said, "You just wait until all of these people are gone. I intend to show you just how much I want you, and only you, tonight."

"I'm about to take a swim," she said dryly and left me standing there.

Before the night was over, each of my boys pinned a couple hundred birthday dollars on Shayla's bikini top. And that was cool, but when Street was pinning his money he had issues getting the pin back on. I watched Shayla's tipsy butt wiggle around as he tried to put the pin back in the material. I didn't know why, but I was bothered by the fact that he had his hands on my wife, and she was enjoying it. Whether intentional or not, him feeling on my wife's breasts was not what was up. I got out of my seat and in his face.

"What's the situation, potna?" I took over the closing of the birthday pin. "Why you lingering around my wife's shit?"

He stepped back and put his hands in the air. He was not only my kinfolks, but my number one, down-for-life general, but I still didn't trust anyone where Shayla was concerned. I looked at Street for an explanation, but Shayla spoke up instead.

"Stop tripping Titus! He was just trying to pin some money on me. I have so much money the pin isn't working anymore." Her words slurred as she spoke. "Plus, we all know that no one up in here would get involved with each other's best friend, would they?"

Her question sounded more like an accusation. Then, she smiled at me like she knew more than she was saying. She gave Street a look that I couldn't quite make out, and added, "Street wouldn't try anything frisky with me. Just like you wouldn't try anything with my friends."

I closed the clasp on the oversized safety pin, and said, "I got it on, but you need another pin. And you're right about Street. I just lose my head about you sometimes."

"Man, it's nothing like that. I was just giving little sis some gwap," Street said.

"Lil sis... humph," I mumbled under my breath and kissed my wife. That woman was my property. No other man should have his hands on her, ever. After breaking away from her soft lips, I asked, "Babe, will you bring me another beer?"

"Anything for you, babe," she said and turned to Street. "Thanks for the money, honey."

When she was completely out of earshot, I gave fair warning. "I'm going to have to watch you, nigga? First, you fiddling with my wife's titties. Next, you'll be over here doing maintenance for her. I ain't got nothing but love for you, mane, but don't think for one minute I'm slow in this motherfucker. I know my wife is fine, but don't get the lines crossed and things will stay copasetic between us."

He knew when I was about that business and when I was about jokes. He said, "No doubt. Bet."

We were about to dap it up when a loud blast almost burst my eardrums. Then, there was a B-d-d-d-d-d-d... POP. POP! POP!

People started screaming, running in different directions, and ducking for cover. The noise was deafening. I searched for Shayla amongst the retreating crowd. When I spotted her underneath a table, I dove on top of her and reached for the nine at my waist-side. I aimed at the man holding a gun and was about to squeeze the trigger when I saw five other guns aiming back at me. That fact didn't bother me; I was born to die. It was the red dots on Shayla's head that made me pause. I dropped my gun and begged, "Don't shoot her, man. It's me you want, so take me instead, please!"

A ski-masked gentleman, who was the leader, said, "We didn't come for blood tonight, only to negotiate."

He pulled me to my feet. Then, he assembled me and my generals in my den for a meeting. As we walked, I made note that most of the people from the party found their way to their cars and left.

At gunpoint, I walked ahead of Street, Tony, Yak, and Buster into the den where the armed men relayed the demands of their Atlanta crime boss, "Big Shirley."

Big Shirley wanted to cut in on my territory, and she sent her goons to lay out her demands. Not only did she want thirty-percent of future profits, she wanted one-point-five million in advance. I slammed my fist on the coffee table.

"If Big Shirley thinks I'm going to work for years to establish a business, and then stand by and watch her bum rush it, she got the whole game fucked up!"

I didn't have the upper hand, but I was ready for war. I would die with honor before I paid to breathe. I was Titus motherfucking Wilson. They were not getting hide or hair of my money. "You'll have to kill me first. Run and tell Big Shirley that!"

The leader stepped so close to me that his Tec-9 pressed against my nose.

"Like I said man, we didn't come for blood tonight, or else you would already be oozing all over this pretty rug. However, if you want to take it there, you can pay up tonight in cash or blood, Mr. motherfucking Wilson," he said.

"I ain't giving you shit!" I told him.

When he saw I wasn't anywhere near ready to be cooperative, he said, "Get his wife in here."

My heart dropped into my drawers when Shayla was thrown into the coffee table so hard that she bumped her side on the corner. She screamed out in pain.

I jumped up and yelled, "You're a dead man!"

When I reached in for the piece in my pocket, the minion that shoved her shot Buster square in the chest. The leader used his gun to shove me back down into my seat.

The leader said, "One more Texas Cowboy move like that and it will be your last. Now you listen, and listen clearly, to the words that are coming out of my mouth. I have clear instructions to get the first one point five tonight. If I don't have it one second after midnight, it will cost you an extra million a day and the blood of someone close to you. Ya heard me? It's a new boss in town, so get used to it."

Visions of the scene in my den flashed before my eyes like a flick. Dark red blood bubbles formed in Busters' mouth as his body jerked feverishly on the recliner. Shayla's contorted face flashed before my eyes. Her eyes winced and her body squirmed in pain. A feeling I had not felt since I moved out of Sloan Mills Projects crept up on me – a feeling of defeat.

Weighing my options, I succumbed to their demands. I'd regroup and hit them back twice as hard.

Or else, once the news got around that my folks were bleeding from another teams' gun and I was paying to keep them off my ass, I'd become an ATM.

"Okay, I'll get you the money," I said, ready to get them out of my house, so we could get Buster to the hospital. The politics of the game were tough. My people's safety was the number one priority – especially baby girl.

"Good choice, young man," he said before a big, ugly, yellow man and a tall, dark-skinned female-looking dude escorted me up to my bedroom's safe. Once his duffle bags were full of cash, they left us all with our face down in the den and vanished out of the side door.

As soon as I heard the door close, I rushed to my gun cabinet looking for my Uzi. I was the first one to run to the door blazing a trail of bullets behind them. Realizing they were on foot made me run even faster to the end of my driveway busting caps left and right.

"Die motherfuckers!" I yelled behind them. But, they made it to their getaway van without one casualty.

When I walked back in the house, Shayla was performing CPR on Buster. I knew he would be dead on arrival, but I instructed Tony and Yak to get him to the emergency room pronto. "Call his family on the way," I told them.

Losing one of my boys in my home did not sit well with me. I couldn't let anyone affiliated with me die on my watch – and definitely not in vain. It was unheard of to hit a boss in his home, assault his wife, kill one of his generals, take his money and then life goes on as usual. There were going to be repercussions. I'd been to war before, but a violation of my sanctuary like that was new to me. Big Shirley could keep the money, but on everything she would repay me in blood. Their blood would be the only source of repayment for Buster, for Shayla, and for the blatant disrespect. I sat there in a vengeful rage for a few minutes after Buster's corpse left for the hospital. My cell phone rang and I didn't recognize the number.

"Who this?"

"It's good to see that we are going to have a lucrative relationship, Titus. Or should I call you Titus motherfucking Wilson?"

"Who is this?"

It sounded like she took a long tug on a cigarette. "First of all, my condolences for your friend... Buster is it? I will send flowers to the funeral home. Second of all, keep the cash flow coming just like you did tonight, and you and your crew will be all right. I'll let you keep your turf, and it will be business as usual, except we're partners now – business partners."

"We are not partners! After I assassinate everyone associated with your no-honor-having crew, I will hunt you down. That's a promise!"

"Oh, simmer down, young man, before you give yourself a heart attack. Sure, we meet under, well, sort of unconventional circumstances, but trust me when I say I plan to introduce myself to you formally. Before we met, I wanted you to feel the fortitude of my force. So, you would know what you were up against, so to speak. Do you feel me? Well, as I said, thanks for making your first payment on time. Sorry it had blood on it, as well, but I need you to know that this is an everyday thing for me. Oh, and when I say that thirty-five-percent is due at the first of every month, I mean that it is due to be paid in full at twelve AM on the first day of every month, and not a minute late."

"I thought it was thirty," I said, not knowing why I was challenging how much I was going to pay her when I didn't plan to pay her one more dime.

"No, that price went up when you shot at my men. Do you see how easy it was for us to touch you in your home? Now that we know that you'll be more prepared next time, we'll simply come harder and when and where you least expect it. Son, I can have a thousand men swarming Lake Nesto in ten minutes, so don't try a Queen like BS." And with that said, all I heard was the dial tone.

My boy Street had listened to the entire exchange on speakerphone. He said, "That's Big Shirley, man. BS stands for Big Shirley. I heard about her when I was doing some transactions in Atlanta. I didn't know she was making her way down this way. With her manpower, she can do just what she says and more. We are up against the big league with her. I think you should pay her."

"Big leagues! I'm not about to let some bitch take by force what I've worked so hard for without a fight. She owes me a million five and to see her blood drip. What you need to be doing is preparing for war."

Chapter 23

Rhonda

I was back in my doctor's office. The stress of the shooting had my stomach tied in knots. I thought it was because of all the things I had on my plate. Regardless of how people think or feel about a mistress, it was hard work to love another woman's husband. If she was your best friend, it was twice as hard.

Anyway, an excruciating pain had taken over my gut, and I'd been getting more and more nauseated. The first time I came to Dr. Swanman's office, they told me I wasn't pregnant, and a tiny bit of relief came over me. I had mixed emotions about having my man's firstborn child. I had to admit that the idea of having Titus' baby made me smile. He was barely talking to me, and when he did, all that he talked about was staying safe. He wanted me to stay out of public as much as possible so that I would be out of harm's way. I loved that he was concerned about me, but not being with him was a serious adjustment I hadn't gotten used to.

The next morning after Shayla's party, Titus went to Atlanta spraying bullets on every corner ran by Big Shirley's squad. She returned the favor on Titus' blocks, as well. He was afraid she would come after the people closest to him next, so he kept checking on me. Sitting in the doctor's office, the more I thought about the whole ordeal, the more my stomach ached. To avert my attention to something else, I picked up the latest Essence of Color Magazine hoping another one of their articles would keep my mind entertained. Just like the first time, the first story I landed on seemed to be directed right at me. It was entitled, *Home Wreckers.*

"Go figure?" I said aloud, knowing it was going to be yet another article bashing the other woman. I wished they would keep it real for once. We all know that it took three to cheat – the unsatisfied husband, his hot ass mistress, and a wife not doing her job at home. For entertainment purposes only, I humored myself and read the article.

Home Wrecking Mistresses

The outcome of being a kept woman is emotional turmoil, spiritual death and merely existing in a realm of misplacement. When a mistress' livelihood depends on her man's stolen time from his wife, she is not living a life of her truest potential..."

The last line sent my stomach back into knots, and I pushed it out of my head. I was not spiritually dead. On the inside, I struggled against a feeling of nostalgia, reminiscent of feelings I had as a child. As a little girl, I yearned for affection and love from my mother when love and affection towards me were the last things on her mind.

Mama was a lively and vibrant lady who worked hard but never seemed to be able to get ahead. When she wasn't working long hours to provide for us, she seemed to get her only source of enjoyment in life by being in the company of different men – many different men. Many of her boyfriends ended up being one-night stands that I hated to see come and go from her bedroom in the wee hours of the morning. That vision haunted me for years afterwards.

The men would make their hasty exit just as the sun threatened to peek up over the horizon outside my window. I'd hear their muted whispers outside my bedroom door in the hallway. Listening to Mama's girlish giggles and the men's empty promises to return, I would turn my face towards the wall as the front door closed behind them. Those men came and went as they pleased, with no ties to Mama, leaving her with nothing but a piece of a memory to hold on to until the next time they decided to show her some more love. Speaking of love, she rarely showed me any type of love or affection that I could feel in my adolescent soul. She'd say I was a strong girl and that I could make it on my own in the world. What she didn't know was that an empty human shell is never strong. It had to be filled with love, joy, and hope to be strong.

I never had that role model to look up to. What I felt every time Mama chose a man over me could not be summed up in words, until she kicked me out of the house over the first man that decided to put a Rent-to-Own ring on her finger.

It was that day that my spirit broke. I told her in words how much I hated her. It was at that point that I lost the ability to genuinely love another female. I mean, *really* love them like family, simply for the beauty of friendship. Due to the fact that the one woman I loved with all that I had in me to love threw me out on the street like a piece of trash for a piece of a man, I was incapable of loving the best friend I ever had. Mama said I had to go, because Mr. Travis didn't feel comfortable with my attitude problem.

When it boiled down to it, a woman was always going to choose her man over another woman, even if she said she loved you. Whether she was your mother, or your so-called Sister-From-Another-Mother, it was always the same. So, I might as well beat her to the punch, and look out for me.

Pushing my dreadful memories of Mama and their relation to my present decision to take my best friend's husband to the back of my mind, I consoled myself with the thought that at least I had someone to love me for real. Well, at least I had a part-time lover that was slowly but steadily working his way into full-time.

Shayla thought she had everything under control, but she had no idea. But, it was the real woman behind the scenes that ran things in relationships. I could do amazing things in the dark, and Titus would come to see the light sooner or later. I flipped the page to read the rest of the eye-opening article just as Dr.

Swanman's blond and bubbly nurse called me to the back.

"So, Ms. Jackson, what's bothering you today?" she asked, once I was sitting in the chair getting my blood pressure taken.

I started to tell her to look at my chart, because the lady at the front desk asked the same question and wrote it there. Instead, I repeated my symptoms to her.

"I'm having really bad stomach cramps. I came in last month, because I thought I needed a new birth control pill since my periods had been irregular. The new pill has me cramping something awful, even worse than before. I've been on three different birth control pills this year, so maybe there is something else wrong with me."

"Have you been under any kind of stress lately?" she asked, writing down notes into my chart.

"Well, I guess you could say that. I was at a party a few days ago, and someone came in shooting. But, I was having pain off and on before then."

"Okay," The nurse looked at me strangely, as if she was judging me for being somewhere that shooting would take place. I really didn't need her condescending attitude then. I was about to tell her so when she took a quick breath, looked back at my chart, and continued, "Well, let's get you checked out. I need you to urinate in one of the cups in the bathroom for a urine sample. Then go to room seven, and remove all of your clothing. Cover yourself with the robe provided on the exam table, and the doctor will be in to see you shortly."

I was perturbed by the way she had looked at me. I had enough people passing judgment on me on a regular basis. I certainly didn't need it from some little petite Barbie look-a-like who had no idea what I had been through – hell, what I was still going through! She was probably born with a silver spoon in her mouth and handed everything to her by her mommy and daddy. I got undressed, hopped up onto the examining table, and covered myself.

Dr. Swanman came in and began his brief examination. As expected, my mouth and ears were clear, and I didn't have any lumps in my breasts. My lungs and heart sounded good, and he said everything looked normal. Since I had just had a pelvic exam and Pap smear the last time I was there, it wasn't necessary this time around. The only thing left was for the phlebotomist to come in and draw some blood so that the doctor could run tests to see if my chemistry was balanced.

I was sure the blood tests were just another way for his office to make some more money, but I wanted to get to the bottom of my pain, so I agreed to it. When the phlebotomist drew my blood and was about to walk out of the room, the doctor and his nurse met him at the door. They were both looking perplexed and nervous, raising my anxiety level up to ten.

Dr. Swanman slowly walked to me and put a hand on my shoulder. He said, "Ms. Jackson, there has been some sort of a mix up in your chart. The last time you were here, your urine pregnancy test was positive, and it read positive again on this visit today. The mix up happened because another patient's test results were erroneously placed into your chart, and your results were placed in hers, thus giving you both false readings." With a look of disgust, he turned to the nurse and said, "Judy, call Mrs. Boutmore right now, and let her know that she is not pregnant."

I'd never heard him address her by her first name before. I raised my eyebrows at the awkward situation. There was a definite cloud of tension in the room. The nurse nodded, shamefully avoiding my stare, with tears welled in her eyes. She quickly left the room. Dr. Swanman shook his head slowly, and then began apologizing.

"Ms. Jackson, I assure you that this type of thing has never happened in my office. It will not happen again. I am so sorry that it happened to you."

"Wait... Are you *sure* that I'm pregnant?" I asked, as my world seemed to start swimming around for a moment. I steadied myself on the exam table with my hands so that I wouldn't fall over.

"This test is pretty much conclusive, but we will know with absolute certainty when your blood tests come back. I'm going to run what we call a serum pregnancy test. This will test the amount of pregnancy hormones in your body. Now, since you have been having irregular periods, we will have to wait a few months and watch the baby's growth before we do an ultrasound to determine how many months you are."

To say that I was in shock would have been an understatement. For some reason, I couldn't comprehend what the doctor had just said. My head wouldn't wrap itself around the idea. Me? Rhonda? Pregnant? My first instinct was to ask what would become of my sexy, well-maintained body. I couldn't picture the possibility of stretch marks and a distended belly. On the other hand, the thought that I was going to be the first one to give Titus a child was exhilarating. There was nothing that sweet little Shayla could do about that!

"Are you sure this is not a mistake, Dr. Swanman?" I asked again, just to be sure I wasn't dreaming.

"Oh, we are sure this time, and like I said, once the serum pregnancy test comes back it will be pretty much conclusive. Right now, let's set you up for a two-week follow-up, and we will call you with the results as soon as we have them."

As Dr. Swanman handed me the instructions on taking care of myself and my baby for the next two weeks, the nurse, who had recomposed herself and joined us a few minutes earlier, handed me a follow-up appointment slip and prenatal vitamins.

Suddenly, she was sweet as sugar. A few minutes ago she was ready to write me off as some ghetto reject, but now that she knew that her job could hinge on my reaction to her obvious mistake, she was all up my ass without lubricant.

"I am very sorry for the mix-up, Ms. Jackson. Thank goodness we caught it when we did. Please make sure that you're back in two weeks."

Everything they said to me about the baby was in slow motion. It was as if they were talking underwater, or something. They kept handing me more bags, bottles, and papers, and I held my hands out for them like a robot. Taking all of the information, introductory care packages, and vitamins, I was in a state of shock and happiness. Sure, I'd been spotting and not having a full period, but I thought that it was because of my birth control pills being changed so often. I had no idea that this was the reason I had been so miserable.

I thought about every time I took a drink in the few months prior. I had been around people smoking and wiling out. Last but not least, I thought about the physical altercation with not only Titus but when his wife attacked me. The safety of my new child had been at stake, and I was completely clueless! On the car ride home, I didn't turn on the radio.

As I turned onto College Street in Auburn toward my apartment complex, I said, "Oh my God! He is going to *have* to love me now. No woman can compare to the mother of his first born child. What man wouldn't love that? I hope we have a son, and we can call him Titus Jr. That would absolutely tear Shayla apart!"

Having Titus' baby would solidify me as a permanent fixture in his life. We were bonded forever by the life growing inside of me. I wouldn't have to worry about whether he would try to get rid of me like he did before I changed his mind in his den. For the next eighteen years, at least, he was mine. *Now, how exactly am I going to break the news to Shayla?*

Chapter 24

Titus

Money can buy a man many things, but it can't buy him respect. That I knew that for a fact, Jack! As I talked to Street, I remembered those valuable words from uncle, Dex. He always told me I was only as strong as my weakest link. I could remember many examples where the people I aligned myself with started out cool, but somewhere down the line they started to look unfamiliar. Well, it turned out that the problem with Big Shirley was a nasty case of betrayal.

I didn't figure it out until my boy transformed into a full-fledged foe. Cutting to the chase, Street was starting to look unfamiliar. First of all, how in the hell did a whole block of corner boys plus a money-drop spot get lit up like the fourth of July two nights in a row? His ass was on location both times, but he was the only one that didn't take a bullet. He was the last man standing to tell the story on both occasions. The first time, I was glad he made it, dapped him up, and even hugged him. I didn't know what I would have done if I lost my boy. But, the second time a block got hit on his watch and he showed up with the bad news without as much as a scratch, I wasn't falling for the okie doke.

Second of all, how was it that he purchased a Jag last week? In the middle of all of the turmoil going on with Big Shirley, my main man was out shopping for cars. We were getting hit left and right, our money was messed up, and he was shopping for high end vehicles. Either that nigga had a real good savings plan with IRAs, savings bonds, and some other shit Obama and 'nem was not telling all the citizens about, or he was skimming off the motherfucking top! I was sure of it.

Third of all, I had it on a reliable source that he was spotted talking to one of the goons that busted up in my house blasting some weeks back. To be seen in the same room as one of those men was an offense punishable by death. But, talking to them was like kissing death in the face. To think he could outsmart me about my money was one thing. However, to think he could align himself with people that had my peeps blood on their hands was some other shit. The concerning part was that he knew my setup, which was probably why it was so easy for them to hit us during Shayla's party in the first place. They had inside information to know when and where we would be the most vulnerable. Several times, when I planned to hit them back hard, they were prepared when we got there. They'd been tipped off.

It had to be Street, I thought reluctantly. Some of the details that Big Shirley knew were so intimate that only my right-hand man knew. I put him to the test by calling him up on his cell phone and told him of a bogus plan about getting back at the other squad. To put the icing on the cake, I told him that I would be there personally to take out that bitch, Big Shirley. An informant had already told me that she showed up at the G-Room every Saturday at 11:45 p.m. sharp.

My goal was to get Street to inform them of a hit on that location, so they would switch up their meeting spot for Saturday. That way, I could follow them to the less populated area, away from the police department, and hit them with the fire.

"Okay, my nigga, you understand we are taking her ass out at the G-room as soon as she walks up in there through the side door at 11:45 sharp!" I gave Street the details. If my inkling was right, he was going to tell her the plan, and my informant would tell me of the new location.

He said, "Aight man. I'm ready for this ho."

"Bet." I was betting his state property, Bitches-R-Us ass hung up the phone and called her right away to snitch. What Street wasn't banking on was the fact that one of the men working close to her was in my pocket, so I would know within an hour where her new spot to collect would be, and I would also find out if my boy was sheisty. Big Shirley thought she was going to be getting another million five from me, but she sincerely had some things to learn about my resilience.

Later that evening, the time came to hit her back hard. As anticipated, Street tipped her off, and they were at their new location. I busted into the room she'd booked at Alabama Suites, and it was twenty-men deep

– all cocked and loaded. That punk nigga, Street, had the nerve to be laying up on the bed counting money. When he saw me, he jumped up and put his hands in the air like I was five-O. Coming through the door gunning, I didn't even hesitate. I put the first two in his disloyal ass.

"Where the fuck is Big Shirley?" I hollered. Without giving them enough time to answer, I put one in the man's chest who was standing by the door and two in the man standing by the bathroom sink. I turned back around quick to catch Street staring at me with wide unblinking eyes. His bullet-riddled body was sprawled across the bed. Thick, congealed blood poured from his gaping mouth. A strong iron smell permeated the room. He had jeopardized not only my business, but my family and the homies, all for what? For the love of money. That gwap scattered all across his chest was worthless blood-splattered confetti.

I would've given him some more paper. He was supposed to be my boy. He was supposed to be… Well, it didn't much matter what he was supposed to be anymore. What he was then was casket-filler. There was no time for regrets or sentiment. Street learned the hard way that there were certain things you just didn't do. Fuckin' with a nigga like Tee was on the top of that list.

My men blasted hard. They took out everyone moving, until I raised my hand signaling them to stop shooting. Then, the desk chair started to swivel and I emptied my clip in it. I didn't see anyone sitting there, so I thought it was a waste of ammo. I lowered my piece.

The chair continued to swivel and I felt like everything was moving in slow motion. I looked over at one of my men, and I saw a shocked look come across his face as the chair turned around. I turned back towards the chair and said, "I'll be damned."

Sitting in that chair was none other than that bitch, Big Shirley. Despite a room full of dead men, she was calm, cool, and collected. She turned all the way around to face me – queen pen to king pen. When the chair made its full circuit and came to a complete halt, I thought my eyes were playing tricks on me. Where the fuck was the rest of this bitch? She was a bonafide midget wearing a little black turtle neck, little jacket, little shoes, and little every damned thing!

Immediately, I felt a tinge of remorse creep up on me. It was bad enough that I was there to check a woman in the first place, but to find out that woman was a midget. I let out an exasperated chuckle and scratched my temple with the warm end of my piece. A few of my men let out nervous laughs, following my lead. Abruptly, I cut off the laughter and scowled at her. I stared her in her beady little midget eyes while silence hung in the air. The tension in the room was suffocating as everyone waited for my next move.

Thinking about the blood that she caused my men to shed, I briskly walked toward her and yanked her out of that midget chair. I mean, I yanked her straight up out of the seat until we were at eye level. Midget or no midget, that trick had caused me serious trouble and heartache, and I wasn't letting up on her just because of her size.

Her feet swung in the air as she turned pale. Gasping for air, she said, "What you gon' do with that gun… besides make me mad?"

I wasn't expecting that mini-monster to be the queen pen of Atlanta.

Lil' Turp yelled, "Just shoot the little bitch, so we can get the hell up out of here." Turp collected the blood money off the bed. He stuffed his pants and a duffle bag that was on the bed.

I said, "I got this, mane. She's responsible for the death of too many of my family and friends, so I'm about to beat this little bitch's ass before I kill her." I commenced to slapping and beating Big Shirley's little bitty midget ass with blows that landed on her left jaw and arm while I held her up with my left arm and punched with the right. She squirmed like a worm on a hook. I only stopped punching her long enough to cock my pistol, ready to put one in her head, and said, "This one is for…"

I had my finger on the trigger, applying pressure, and pop almost went the weasel. Then, I heard a word that I hadn't heard in all the time I had been slanging drugs. That one word made me sorry I hadn't taken the bitch out when I'd had the chance.

"FREEZE!" I dropped Big Shirley and she landed with a hard thump on the thinly carpeted floor. We were surrounded by SWAT.

Big Shirley wiggled her fat fingers into her pocket, whipped out her badge, and said, "Yeah, freeze, punk!

You're heading downtown for murder, distribution of a controlled substance, and any other charges I can think of on the way to the station. Now drop your gun!"

The question of whether or not I should take her out where she stood, or cooperate with the police surrounding me, ran through my mind a few seconds before I dropped the gun, knowing that I was defeated.

She jumped up from the floor and slapped a set of handcuffs on my wrist and read me my rights. "You have the right to remain silent. Anything you say, or do, can and will be used against you in a court of law..."

Chapter 25

Gladys

"Hey DJ, keep playing that song, of mine, all night. On and on and on..." was playing over and over in my mind. I was getting ready to make a major move with one of my most important clients, but my mind was a thousand miles away.

My assistant, Lissa, and I worked late to get everything prepared for the client. With thoughts of Mav dancing through my mind, I found myself sitting in my chair, dancing to the beat of our drum. Closing my eyes, I rested my head on the back of my leather executive chair and began to fully relax.

Lissa was preoccupied with files that I dropped off on her desk. Therefore, I took advantage of the few extra moments to let my mind roam free. I could see Maverick and we were singing the sweet notes of our special songs. The mental and physical energy generated within me as I melted into his strong arms was unbelievable. Vitality shot through my body. I let out a shaky sigh of ecstasy. I was fully aware that if

Lissa was to walk in on me during that moment, I would look completely crazy, but I didn't care. It was what I needed to relax. I was a business powerhouse, but in his arms, I was completely spent.

After he dipped and swung me around gracefully to the enchanting words of Always and Forever, my mind was in a whirlwind of wander. Rhythmic vibrations threatened to fade away into the winds of indifference. I attempted to speak, but was barely able to exhale the words, "Baby, don't let this song come to an end." When I could no longer hear Luther Vandross' vibrant voice in my head, I sent up a silent prayer to the only person I knew that could create a miracle and make this dream a reality.

"Jesus Cristo, please let that groove continue. Amen, así sea..." That trip down memory lane was so real. I didn't want that sweet song to end. My feet rocked left to right in front of my chair. I imagined Mav and I sliding across the floor doing our own rendition of the e-e-electric slide! I slid further into ecstasy when he dipped me again, like a skilled performer, and guided me through this heated dance. He was truly the commander of that symphony. With my hands tightly clutching the arms of my chair, I'd sat at my desk for a full fifteen minutes recapturing our time together. I imagined our tongues doing the tango so well that I knew when I saw him again, our next kiss would be explosive. The world disappeared completely as I left my physical body to join Maverick. With his spirit and my soul, we became one in every possible way. I rubbed my arms with my hands, savoring the feeling. I loved it when I daydreamed about Maverick. The way he held me in my dreams was a blessing straight from above. I was in love with him and the idea of rekindling our love. Our precious memories were captured and held steady in mi corazon and my spirit, which I replayed over and over. With an aura of happiness all around me, I opened my eyes.

Just as I snapped out of my dream, a loud object slammed down onto my desk.

"Bitch! I know you heard me!"

It took a few seconds for my vision to focus and see Lissa standing beside James looking as if she feared for her life. He had one fist on my desk and his free hand pointed at my face.

"James, what are you... what do you want?" I wondered how he was able to clear security, since he was on the no-contact list at Naytek. The security guard downstairs must had been slipping.

A week ago, I backed a small U-Haul up to the house and loaded up everything I could get inside of it in less than two hours. I didn't take furniture or anything, just things the kids and I would need.

Lissa interrupted, "Mrs. LaQuinn. I tried to tell *Mr.* LaQuinn that he didn't have clearance to be in here." She clearly was afraid.

"If you know what's good for you, you'd get back to your desk," he said to Lissa. Yanking me clean out of my chair, he said, "So, you think you are just going to leave me? I will kill you first." He raised his closed fist in the air, and I just knew that I'd be getting wheeled out of my office into somebody's hospital before the evening was over.

The fact that he invaded that sacred space was inconceivable. That was my office – the place where I ruled the roost. He showed his ass in front of Lissa, who had looked up to me at work. I felt the epitome of shame. All of my emotions fought for precedence within me – anger for being violated, fear and anxiety over what James was about to do, and shame and humiliation for it occurring in front of one of my subordinates. I swallowed the large gulp of air caught in my throat.

Through a trembling voice, I said, "Please, James, don't do this here."

"Please, James, don't do this here? Look what you are doing to us," he mocked me.

I realized that his fist was still cocked and loaded. On the horizon, there were so many possibilities for me. But, with James nipping at my heels, constantly dragging me down, I didn't know how I was going to get away. I'd shrunk into the bottomless pit of sorrow that he dug for me all the years that I'd been his wife. I gave up, until I heard the voice of light pierce through the cloud of despair.

"If you don't get your hands off my lady!" Maverick said, coming through the door just as security arrived to apprehend James. He tossed the flowers he had in his hands onto the floor. Reaching James before security, he punched him square across the jaw.

James' neck cocked back and he hit the floor.

"You have no right to put your hand on a woman like that. You are less than a man. You're dirt! And if I catch you around her again, it's going to be worse."

He walked around the desk and came to my side as security pulled James to his feet.

Maverick put an arm around me and said to James, "This lady right here, is mine. Pay attention long enough, and I'll show you how to treat her, and your kids."

With the mention of our kids, James squirmed around trying to get out of the hold of security. Instead of directing any of his venom toward Maverick, he called me all sorts of bitches.

"You can have her. She never was nothing, and she'll never be anything. Remember, if she cheated on me, she'll cheat on you!" he told Maverick.

That man had beaten me down in every possible way, physically and mentally. He cheated on me with more women than I could even count. Yet there he stood, accusing me of being the one who broke our wedding vows. I was glad that Mav's strong arms comforted me. I was afraid I would collapse on the spot if he let me go. He didn't say anything as security carted James out of the room to be held for the police.

The head of security said, "Mrs. LaQuinn, in a few minutes, I will need everyone to come to the security office to give a statement to the police."

I nodded and made brief eye contact with my secretary. I searched her face for any trace of judgment or disgust, but all I saw was pure concern. I smiled weakly at her and mouthed the words, "Thank you."

She nodded and smiled encouragingly. Pointing towards Maverick, she raised her eyebrows and shot me a thumbs up sign. I smiled as she walked out and closed the door behind her.

Once everyone was out of the room, Maverick's tilted my head upwards, looked over my face and neck as if he was expecting to see bruises.

"Are you okay?" he asked, as he pulled me gently into his arms for a strong embrace.

"Yes, now that you are here." I let him hold me as I cried.

"Gladys." He dropped down on one knee. "I want to make sure that starting today, no man will ever put his hands on you. While I know you are his wife on paper, I know you are not his wife in your heart. After all these years, the love we share has never lost its zeal. I care for you today the same way I did in college, but multiply that by a thousand and you have the way I feel for you now. Before I came in here and saw that piece of a man you've been dealing with, I planned to give you this, but now this is all the more important."

He opened a jewelry box and inside was a beautiful gleaming ring.

"I'm not saying let's get married, but I am promising you that I intend to do just that, when the time is right," he said.

My heart fell into my stomach and I shook uncontrollably. I couldn't hold back the waterfall. In a range of twenty minutes, I'd gone from daydreaming a sweet love song about Maverick, to a fight with James, and back to Maverick showering me with his unconditional love.

"I accept! I accept!" I said and leaned down to kiss his face. He stood up and leaned in for a tender moment. Breaking the kiss, I said, "You've made me happier than you'll ever know. You've just made all of those dreams come true. Thank you. Now, will you go to the security office with me? I don't have the strength to face James alone."

"As long as there is breath in my body, you will never have to face him alone again. Lead the way baby." He took my hand in his and walked me towards my office door.

After talking to security, I pressed charges against James. I went back to my office, cleaned my desk, and Maverick and I left. The CEO personally stood in on the security meeting and suggested I take the rest of the week off. Once I closed the deal I was working on, I would definitely take the time off. Lissa was at her desk when I exited my office.

"Please forward all calls to your cell for the weekend, and only call me if there is an emergency that you can't handle. We'll get back on this proposal first thing Monday," I said to her.

"Sure thing. Do you need me to do anything else?"

"No, that will be all."

"Oh, Mrs. LaQuinn… I'm so sorry he got in…"

"It is not your fault, so don't worry about it, Lissa. Have a nice weekend."

"You too," she said dropping her head down into the work in front of her as I walked by. She really had no reason to feel bad. James was the one who caused the trouble. I knew what it felt like to feel responsible for something that was not your fault, so I turned back around to address her.

"Lissa, James is the one with the problem, not us. Thank you for being there to call security for me, and thank you for taking care of everything while I am gone."

"You're welcome, Gladys. Have a wonderful weekend."

Maverick and I walked out of the office, hand in hand.

***

The first week after I left James, the kids and I stayed with my mother. Mav and I had spoke on the phone every night. We decided to take it slow. That was until he showed up at my job with the promise ring and saw James there. After the display that he witnessed in my office, he said he definitely would not spend another day or night without being close to me, so that he could protect me. What he didn't know was that I was preparing to be closer to him, too.

I talked to my boss and negotiated opening a new office in Miami. Once those plans were final, I rented an apartment downtown, so I could be close to Maverick's home. I didn't want the kids to be too traumatized with me leaving their father and moving in with a new man so fast. So, while I wanted to move in with him more than I wanted my next breath, for the kids' sake, I got our own apartment.

Walking through my mother's door, I greeted Nazaria and Kelvin. They were in their makeshift play room, which had previously been Mother's sewing room. She quickly rearranged the room for them when we moved in, so they could have a place to play. My babies were playing quietly, and Mother was right by their side, attempting to read a book. I stood in the doorway and watched them play for a few minutes. I took in the essence of three of the most important people in my life.

At that moment, I was full of peace, serenity, hope, and encouragement. Finally, they had the harmony they deserved. I had the love that I'd always craved, and with Maverick, I had all the joy my heart could muster. Sure, my not-so-typical journey to happiness had bumpy roads – lots of them. Yet, each bump was necessary for my ultimate outcome. I wouldn't be the strong woman I was without going through all that I had went through with James. Each blow that he dealt taught me something new about myself. I learned what a resilient person I could be. I learned that I could go through the very worst storm and come out the other side better than ever.

Chapter 26

Rhonda

The day after my doctor's appointment, I was itching to tell everyone the news of the bundle of joy growing inside of me. I called my mother to tell her, along with a host of other family members. My mother didn't answer, which was typical. She probably was spending time with Mr. Travis.

I hadn't got around to telling Gladys, or the two most important people – Shayla and Titus. I was saving them for last. I was sick and tired of tiptoeing around Shayla. And, I couldn't wait to see Titus' face when I gave him the news. I dialed his cell phone more than a few times in the past few days with no answer. I knew he was dealing with the pressing issues he had with Big Shirley. However, the information I had to put in his ear would trump it all. After the fifth unanswered call to his cell, I left a voice message.

"Titus, baby, I really need to talk to you. I have some great news for you... for us. Be safe out there, babe, and call me as soon as you can." I pressed END on my cell phone, plopped down onto my bed, and rubbed my stomach.

There is really a growing baby inside of me, I thought about the reality of carrying Titus' child. When I thought about my Shayla, the memories we shared – all the times we went shopping together, wore each other's clothes, popped popcorn at three in the morning, or fixed each other's hair for a date – I got sad.

All of those precious memories flashed through my mind as I contemplated sending her a text message to let her know that I was pregnant by her husband. With all the happiness I felt about the blessing growing inside of me, I didn't have the courage to dial her number to deliver the words that would devastate her life as she knew it. I could not face her woman to woman.

As my hand traveled over the contours of my stomach, I came to the realization that I had a bigger priority than Shayla to worry about now. I had to think of my baby. I had to send her the text and let her know, so that Titus and I could effectively start our life together. Of course I would have rather have told Tee before Shayla. However, he was out of contact, so I told the next person in line.

"Oh, well, here goes nothing," I whispered in the quietness of my bedroom. I pulled out my Blackberry and composed the message I knew would impact my friend's life in a massive, negative way. I felt a feeling that I hadn't felt during all of the nights of hot passion and morning quickies I'd had with her husband – guilt.

My text read:

I want you to believe me when I say that I truly hate to tell this in a text. Titus and I are in love; we really are. I still love you like a sister, BUT I love Titus in a way that I have never loved anyone. I just found out that I'm pregnant and he is the father. I hope that in some way we can find a way to reconcile our friendship, so you can be in the baby's life. We always said that when we each had children we would be each others child's Godmother. I don't want the fact that this is Titus' child to change that. I do regret that things turned out the way that they did, but as you once said, we can't help who we love. Titus and I will be together in the end. I know that for sure.

P.S. Call me when you are ready to talk about this.

I pressed SEND on my phone without a moment's hesitation, and the message went off into text messaging oblivion, soon to arrive on Shayla's cell phone exposing all of my dirty little secrets. I was comforted by the honesty and purity that would grow from that action. No more lies. No more games. Everything was on the line for all involved to take note, deal with it, and hopefully move on peacefully. I exhaled a sigh of relief as the message uploaded and cleared my cell phone's screen. At that moment, my complete hand was exposed, but I was keeping it real with my sister. I sat on the edge of the bed and felt like I was getting a little lightheaded. The air seemed to be filling my lungs too slowly to provide oxygen to my brain as fast as I needed it. I felt my heart pounding like a bass drum in my chest. My eyes grew wide as I looked over at the Blackberry in a panic anticipating her response. She didn't send me one.

The message was sent and delivered. There was no turning back. No matter how I tried to console myself, I knew that I had unequivocally let my friend down. Some old woman once told me that the truth would set me free, but at that very moment I begged to differ. I felt like I was locked in a bird cage singing chain gang blues, wishing, and hoping to one day be free of my sins. Many nights I laid in the dark with her man, enjoying the fruits of her labor, and not caring the least bit how my actions would affect her. I hadn't even thought about all of the years she had looked out for me when my own mother had tossed me aside. With that thought, a feeling of utter shame came over me. My gaze fell to the floor, and I could feel my shoulders hunching up and down. I didn't realize I was crying until uncontrollable tears soaked my shirt. Was I really crying about indulging in an affair I craved so much? Was Titus' baby growing in my stomach a reason for sorrow? Was the message I'd just sent to my friend in the best interest of everyone involved?

I thought sending her the message would make me feel better. If that was true, why did I feel like I'd just been hit by a transfer truck?

Chapter 27

Titus

Lee County be trippin' once you hit the county jail! It was one month after I got locked down in that hell hole of a jail cell, and I had gone through a hell of a lot of money on my books, red tape, pre-trials, court hearings, and lawyer fees. I had set myself up where my hands were practically clean of the actual murders or drug deals, but the DA was trying to stick every crime in the city from the last five years in my file. The cops, lawyers, and judges that I thought for sure I had in my pocket were all talking that same shit about their hands being tied. What had I paid them all of those years for? I made a memo to fire all their fake people-in-high-places asses ASAP. I realized that it wasn't until the shit really hit the fuckin' fan that you found out who you really had on your team.

My lawyer that I'd been down with since day one, Klint Kasashki, called in a slick cat from Chicago to figure out the loopholes in my case. It was then that I finally was able to get out on a one-million-dollar bond.

A million dollars!

That bond put a serious dent in my cash flow that already seemed to be dwindling. The numbers from the streets were not adding up right since I'd been gone. Nevertheless, I was fresh out of the county and ready to get back to business. When I was escorted up to the front to check out, I noticed my cousin, Jay, standing at the release counter to pick me up.

"What's up, my nig?" I asked him.

"Nothing much, man."

"Yo, where is Lil' Red?"

I had sent word from lockup that my next-in-command, Lil' Red, was supposed to be handling my business while I was gone. Since the money had been funny, and that nigga didn't show up to get me from jail, I knew there was some serious business to take care of on the home front. I had to show folks I was still about the business.

"He had some business to take care of, so he sent me," Jay said, looking as if he had something real serious on his mind. He avoided eye contact and tapped his cigarette box onto his hand. Taking out a cigarette, he lit it and took a long drag. As I looked at him suspiciously, he asked the woman behind the counter, "Is he good to go?"

I got all kinds of bad vibes from my cousin. He normally didn't act funny like that. I wanted answers, but that wasn't the time or the place.

Once the woman said, "You're free to go, Mr. Wilson," I immediately asked Jay, "What kind of business could Lil' Red have had to take care of that he couldn't come and pick me up?"

Jay simply shrugged as we walked out of the building to the car. That shit smelt foul and somebody was going to come up with some answers in this piece.

I hopped in the driver's side of my SC10 and peeled out of the courthouse parking lot with a gang of unanswered questions dangling in the air. I had so much on my mind that I didn't know which direction to go in first. I guessed the first thing I needed to do was find Lil' Red and find out what was good with my paper. Then, I'd collect loose money floating around with my generals.

It didn't go over my head that Jay sat there on the passenger seat, quietly looking out of the window puffing on that cigarette like it was the last one ever made. He was a ticking time bomb. I looked over at him for a good minute once we were at a stop light. He was uncomfortable, which made me uncomfortable.

The light turned green and the car behind me blared their horn, and then skidded from behind my car and shot past us on the left. I sat right where I was, with my foot pressing hard on the brake, looking dead at Jay.

He looked up at the light and then quickly looked at me. We wasn't going nowhere until I got some answers. As far as I was concerned, we could sit in that car all day. My cousin knew he'd better start talking fast. He took one last drag off his cigarette, and said, "Shayla is gone, man."

He watched my house while I was in jail, as he had been instructed to do. I didn't know if someone would take it upon themselves to retaliate against my family while I was locked up, so I couldn't be too careful. He told me that, in the process of watching my place, he noticed that Shayla moved her things out of our home. Through a good source, he found out she had an apartment in Columbus and that some Spanish guy helped her move. I was silent for a minute. Jay looked back out of his window.

"Yeah, right!" I cracked a little giggle, just to make him feel good for trying to amuse me. I started the car rolling forward again, turning my head forward towards the road. I kept waiting for him to get to the punch line, or at least tell me that if she had moved, she was smoking crack, as well. I knew good and well that *my wife* had to be on something serious if she thought that the news of her letting some random dude pack her up and move her to another city was going to go over without repercussions.

That's when I remembered that she'd only been to the jailhouse to see me twice the whole time I was in county. I didn't find it too strange at the time, because I told her not to worry about coming to visit me and to hold herself together until I got out. I assured her that everything would be all right and told her to keep living her life. Little did I know that living her life apparently meant living it – without me.

On the other hand, once Rhonda had found out where I was, she was up there every chance she got for visitation. I knew she would have been worried about me, and I was right. She told me that she had been trying to call and text me for weeks to tell me the big news about her baby. That was the thing about Rhonda. She cared and she always kept it 100. She held a brother down. In fact, I probably would have been more surprised if Jay told me that *she* was seeing someone else while I was in lockdown. In all the time I'd been messing with her, I never saw another guy around her. I had to give her credit for loyalty. I was so caught up in the drama about the charges and the baby that I hadn't even thought about what Shayla was up to.

When she told me she was pregnant, I wanted to punch something. I told her not to tell Shayla until I got out. I didn't want her to find out that we were expecting a child while I was away in jail.

Shit! What if Rhonda told her? I slammed my fist into the steering wheel, causing Jay to jump in his seat.

"Hey, man... calm down, Tee!" he exclaimed, snapping his seatbelt into place.

Ignoring him, I fumed, thinking about the possibility that Rhonda would be stupid enough to tell Shayla our business when I told her not to say a word and that I would handle it once I got out.

Between my case and the bombshell news Rhonda had dropped on me about the baby, Shayla's not visiting seemed like a blessing in disguise. I was happy that she didn't come to see me much while I was locked down, like an animal in a cage, with a secret baby waiting for me once I got out. Interrupting my thoughts, Jay continued to be a bearer of bad news.

"Well, shit, Tee, since you're pissed off already... There is really no good way to say this, man, so I'm just going to give it to you straight, no chaser. The word is that Shayla is taking company with that Hispanic guy Tanya goes to school with. One thing I know for sure is that he did talk her into getting away from the entire situation once Rhonda sent her that text message about your baby being on the way..."

I shut my eyes and put my head down on the steering wheel. I couldn't be losing my wife. I loved that woman to death. I meant, I really loved her *to death.*

"Do you want me to drive?" Jay asked.

I put the car in park, and within seconds I had him by the front of his shirt. That time we were on a residential street, and there was no traffic. I leaned into the passenger's seat with my face inches in front of Jay. "You better have your story straight, man!"

Jay knew the consequences of darkening my first lady's name without sufficient evidence. He watched me pistol whip a corner boy for simply whistling at her before. The poor cat hadn't known what hit him when I gripped that nine and busted his lip open to the white meat. Cousin or no cousin, Jay could only imagine what I would do if his accusation about wifey cheating and moving out of our home with some guy wasn't legit.

I watched his eyes get real wide, exposing the redness. He searched for the best way to let me know that the man I'd hired to clean my pool was also providing therapy sessions to my wife.

"Come on, cuz! You're acting like I messed with her or something," he said, aggravated with my frustration.

He yanked his shirt from my hands and pushed me away from him. "I'm just bringing you up to speed on what's been going on since you've been in."

I rubbed the top of my head and rocked back and forth in the seat. Jay readjusted himself, and I could hear his heavy breathing slow down to a regular pace. He turned again and looked out of the window, again.

Finally, I said, "I just got out the county. I'm tired, hungry, and ready to see my wife. Kinfolk, you could have came and told me this as soon as it happened."

I put my hand on his pistol that was at his side in the seat, and said, "Now, turn your punk ass around, and look at me when you speak. Start from the fuckin' beginning. You're making me nervous with all that cigarette puffing and looking crazy."

"Take a look at this security video from Tanya's house from about three weeks ago."

He pulled a DVD from his back pocket and handed it to me.

"I think that you'll find all of the evidence that you need on the video to confirm what I'm trying to tell you. Also, look at the video from your house two weeks ago when she moved out," he said.

I sneered at him angrily. I wished he would just finish the story, instead of giving me a DVD. I took the DVD and slowly slid it into the built-in DVD player in my car. I braced myself for whatever was to come.

Chapter 28

Shayla

When I received that text about Rhonda's baby, my whole mind went blank. I felt like the Earth stopped spinning on its axis. It was like all of the nightmares I had been afraid of for so long decided to come true all at once. I couldn't think of the first step to take, or even the first thought to think. I couldn't call my family. They would say I told you so. I couldn't call Gladys. She was dealing with her own mess. I couldn't call Rhonda. She was the enemy. I sat down at my kitchen table and stared off into space.

In a daze, I picked up my house phone. I called Antonio. He'd given me so much encouragement and advice while Titus was in jail. I had to admit that having him show genuine care and concern the way that he did at a time when I was at my very lowest caused me to start having feelings for him. After being betrayed by two people in my life, having someone new show true kindness was exactly what I needed. I allowed him to comfort me.

Regardless of how amazing he was, I didn't want a rebound man. More importantly, I didn't know how Titus was going to react to the news that I had moved out of our home while he was locked up. His reaction was at the top of my list of worries. When he touched his feet on free soil, he was going to want answers as to why I was not at home. I knew my husband, and he wasn't the type to let something like this go. He was used to getting what he wanted, but he would never get me back – ever. Getting Rhonda pregnant was the final straw. I'd be damned if I was going to play stepmother and godmother to their child!

Despite the things running through my mind, I was aware of Antonio standing in my new kitchen cooking dinner. "Te quiero. Te amo, Shayla. Mi Amor. Quiero pasar el resto de mi vida contigo. Te quiero con toda mi alma," he said in response to my ambivalence to open up to him.

My Spanish was sketchy, but I knew the meaning of those words. He wanted me? He loved me? He wanted to spend the rest of his life with me, and he wanted me with all of his soul?

It was all so overwhelming. Had I lost my ability to love? Had those two heartless people ruined me? Would I be able to trust my heart with someone again? Though I felt it was to soon to start another relationship, those questions were real to me.

I sat back in my chair, folded my arms across my chest, and hot tears rolled down each of my cheeks.

"Antonio, if I give you a chance, promise you will not disrespect me. Just promise to be the same man five years from now that you are today."

He turned down the burners and gave the food one last stir. Moving away from the delicious smelling pots on the stove, he walked over and stood in front of me. He gently wiped away my tears. His look of sincerity was so pure that I didn't second-guess him.

"I promise," he said, leaning in to kiss my lips.

"You deserve a woman who is husband and drama free. I cannot give you that, right now," I said.

My gaze fell to the floor. My heart was in limbo, caught between going back through the same raggedy door that I was used to, or opening a new shiny door to experience new possibilities.

He pressed his finger against my lip hushing my negative thoughts. Slowly lifting me out of my seat to stand eye to eye with him, he whispered, "I deserve you. You just have to let me to love you."

The barriers I built to protect my heart from ever loving again were slowly melting away. But, would this feeling last long enough to start over?

***

One week later, I moved tirelessly about my new apartment. Although my energy level was zero, I unpacked boxes and arranged new furniture in my new cozy place. I knew that they said not to kick a man when he was down, but leaving Titus behind was the best thing I could have done. After the heartache I had endured, I was determined to get my life back in order. No sooner than I'd written off that part of my life, my cell phone rang and it was Titus' cell number. I dropped the phone like a hot potato. His calling could only mean one thing – he was out of jail and looking for me.

Avoiding him would only make matters worse, so I decided to just answer his call to give us both the closure that we needed. Though I was a bundle of nerves, my voice was firm.

"Hello, Titus."

"Don't *'Hello, Titus'* me! Where are you?"

"I'm at my apartment."

"I need you to come back home, baby. I miss you, and I'm sorry for everything – me getting locked up... the baby." I heard him inhale, holding his breath. He actually had an air of sincerity in his voice.

I could feel my stomach tie up in knots. Yes, I had already gotten the text, but to hear him confirm his relationship with Rhonda was enough to solidify our divorce. I paced my bedroom floor and then walked out into the hallway for more walking space.

My voice shook as I told him, "No, Titus, you don't *need* anything from me. You never have. What you *need* is to take care of your child and give me a chance to find true happiness with someone who knows how to appreciate me."

Obviously the thought of my happiness with another man jarred something in him, because he raised his voice and said, "What's up with this Hispanic fool? What makes you think you can cheat on me?"

"What made you think you could get my best friend pregnant and help ruin a friendship I had since I was a child? What makes you think you can call me and talk about how much you need me now? You didn't need me when you were between Rhonda's legs, so why need me now? You didn't need me when you turned into a big shot and could never find your way home, so why need me now? You didn't need me once you got your business kicked off, and the money started rolling in! I was less than a woman to you then, so why need me now? Besides, I'm not cheating on you, because your divorce paperwork is in the mail. Sign them, and then you need to take care of your baby!"

"Shayla." He sighed, struggling to find his next words. "I'm sorry, baby. I know you've heard it before, but not like this. I am very sorry for the way I treated you and for raising my voice. I know Rhonda told you about her baby, but that baby might not even be mine. You should think about it. You could be throwing our marriage away for nothing, Shay. For real."

"Might? Might means it might *be* yours. It *means* you were *there* in position to be a potential father of the child, and I don't want any part of my husband being a possible father to another woman's child. That doesn't work for me, Titus. *You* should think about *that!*"

I continued to pace the hallway floor, rubbing my throbbing temples to relieve the pain shooting through my head. How in the world did I end up having this conversation with my husband? In what world is this normal? His utter disrespect of our marriage, the new baby with Rhonda, the constant fear of police raids, or even worse, the next "Big Shirley" that would inevitably surface if Titus continued his current lifestyle, was just not worth it. Of course, there was a time when I would have risked it all just to be able to spend my life with him. That was when I felt that it was me and him against the world.

He blew a long breath into the phone. "Okay, Shay. I'll admit that I really messed up this time. I hope you find it in your heart to, at least, forgive me. We have a lot of history together and, I don't know, somewhere down the line things got messed up."

That time when he spoke it didn't sound like game. It honestly sounded as if he hoped that one day we could see eye to eye again. I could respect that.

"You are already forgiven. Money and power has the ability to change people, especially when they aren't used to it. I just can't live like that anymore. I never disrespected you the entire time we were married, yet I took disrespect from you on a daily basis. I honestly hope that you and Rhonda are able to find something to love in each other."

With the mention of my husband and friend as a couple, those were my final words to him. I pressed END on my cell phone and walked into my bedroom. In order to keep my mind occupied, I hung clothes in the closet.

When Titus apologized instead of acting a fool, I felt relieved and hopeful that that phase of my life was coming to a peaceful close. I'd been beaten down for so long by his trifling ways that getting it all out in the open was a relief. I was tired of the lies, tired of the deceit, and tired of the pretending. I was more than tired – I was exhausted. I didn't want revenge. I just wanted them to leave me alone. It was funny how God had a way of bringing us all back to square one. Living in the midst of chaos had taken me a long way during my spiritual journey. Going through adversity puts you in a different place. It reminds you of what is important in life. I turned on the radio and popped in Yolanda Adams' CD, *Never Give Up*.

I praised God. I was happy with His blessings, and that was worth more than a thousand chinchilla's and diamond rings.

THE END

ORDER PART TWO NOW

Secrets of a Kept Woman 2

Also Available by Shani Greene-Dowdell

Keepin' It (Love) Tight (Novel)

Lord, Why Does It Feel So Good? (Short story)

Before the Clock Strikes Twelve (Short Story)

Mocha Chocolate: Taste a Piece of Ecstasy

(Multi-Author Anthology)

Mocha Chocolate: Escapades of Passion

(Multi-Author Anthology)

Savor: The Longest Night

(Multi-Author Anthology)

Made in the USA
Charleston, SC
07 June 2015